ALL I WANT FOR CHRISTMAS ARE MY TWO FRONT FANGS

JD Nelson

To Nels, always Nels

CHAPTER ONE

What do we want?

No humans!

When do we want it?

Now!

I rolled onto my side and pressed my pillow over my ear. It did nothing to block out the chants of the gaggle of sharp-toothed neighbors that were marching around on my front lawn. Nothing could. Some days you just wanted to wake up in another house, in another town, on another planet.

Vampires … they could be so damn dramatic.

Don't get me wrong. I wasn't completely unfeeling toward the advanced persons of our population. Indeed, there were several vampires I loved as much as any of my human friends. However, and this was a big freakin', however, vampires could be pushy and self-entitled. Like, ridiculously over the top pushy and self-entitled. I could hardly blame them for it. I mean, I could imagine there's a point in which even the most steadfast of humanist vampires tire of the constant barrage of people trying to stake them.

For that reason alone, it made sense that vampires would want a safe haven, would want to be able to live in peace without the worry of attack. That sanctuary, at least for the vampires of Virginia, was the town of Everlast.

Everlast, like all vampire settlements, was originally a small human town. Only two short years ago, it was known as Peach, Virginia. Peach was my hometown. I'd spent every second of my twenty-two years inside the city limits. Even after I graduated from our tiny junior college, I didn't have any big city aspirations. If you

1

asked me, there was something comforting about living in a town whose only claim to fame was prizewinning peach preserves and southern hospitality.

Everyone in Peach knew who I was. They knew where I lived, who my family was, and how many years I'd worked at the post office. Hell, most were probably present at my birth. Why on Earth would I ever want to live anywhere else? Peach was my home.

Unfortunately, the only thing left of the quaint, touristy charm that one would associate with a mecca for jam aficionados is me, Sapphire Dragulj, and my house. Everything else had been replaced by thousands of matching stucco townhouses, three Olympic sized swimming pools, two golf courses, and if they had their way with my property, a dozen tennis courts and a fancy clubhouse.

Most people (and vampires) wondered why I was so reluctant to leave Everlast, and believe me, sometimes I wondered myself, but really, I think it all boiled down to me not being able to bring myself to leave the house my great-grandfather built with his own two hands ... to give it up, like it never meant anything to anyone.

I just couldn't do that. My grandmother had loved this house. She grew up here, and when her father died, she had made it her own, from the white eyelet curtains that still hung in the kitchen, to the welcoming garden full of narcissus and roses out front. I didn't want to lose all that or anything that reminded me of my grandparents. All of that gone, just so that they could put in tennis courts—tennis courts I wouldn't be allowed to use because I was, quote-unquote, life-challenged? Thanks, but no thanks.

Life-challenged ... ugh. I hated that term. It was the politically correct term for us lowly human blood bags, more commonly known as 'donors'. The arrival of that priceless gem of a phrase came when the anti-human segment within the vampire population protested a murder that their leader (Everlast's creator and the bane of my existence), Kieran Kinane, was arrested for.

For a while, I couldn't walk down the street at night without a vampire harassing me. I learned then that there are a plethora of degrading slurs and fun-filled gestures a vampire could use when faced with the horrifyingly scary threat of a human woman. My personal favorite was the combo of a slow drag of a thumb across a neck and the words, "You're dead, blood bag," through sharpened fangs. Nothing makes you feel warm and fuzzy like death threats from your neighbors.

There were quite a few stakings and even more human deaths before a compromise was finally met at Kinane's mockery of a trial. We were all, vampires and humans alike, glad when it ended, though we all knew that Kieran going free was a bullshit ruling.

Humans may be the weaker race, but we aren't stupid. We understand that we can't control vampires. It would take only one of them to silently massacre an entire neighborhood. Kieran obviously couldn't be convicted of his crime because he was the only one that could keep his people in check, but, on the other hand, we humans needed a way to save face too, else we'd appear easy to maneuver. Virginians wouldn't stand for that. Thus, the term, 'life-challenged' was born.

It was the perfect distraction from the murder case. Humans knew it wouldn't stop the occasional torture and death of their kind, but it would now be considered a hate crime, and to them, that was worth letting Kieran go free.

What do we want?

No humans!

When do we want it?

Now!

I grabbed another pillow, put it on top of the other one, and gritted my teeth against their ridiculously uncreative demonstration. You'd think vampires would come up with something a little more original than that tired old rhyme and employ a slightly scarier tactic to get me out of the neighborhood, but no. All I knew for sure was that I was going to have to get a night job if they kept this up.

***

When the sun finally made its appearance over the top of the Blue Ridge Mountains, so did my friend, Alexis. "Wakey! Wakey!" she shouted through the screen door.

I unlatched the old-fashioned lock and handed Alexis a cup of her favorite hazelnut coffee. "What do you mean, 'Wakey! Wakey!'? I'm obviously awake if the door is open, genius."

"Don't sass your ride, Miss Ma'am," she countered. "I can let you walk to work, you know."

I gasped in mock horror. "You wouldn't."

"Sure will. The whole two blocks."

"How can you sleep at night?"

She laughed at our usual joke. "Easy, I don't."

Alexis had become my best friend almost the moment she stepped into the Everlast post office. That day, I talked to her about the merits of the Forever stamp, explaining that her new husband would be around … well, forever, and she, in turn, invited me to lunch to thank me for pointing out the error of her mailing ways. Now, a year and a half later, we're BFF's and pretty much inseparable during the daytime when I'm not working … and sometimes when I am working. Apparently, being the wife of someone who was dead during the day could be very boring.

Though Alexis and I were both human and the same age, that's where our similarities ended. Her vampire husband, Ronan, once said that we got on so well because we are opposites of one another. He elaborated on this dream-crushing statement in the best possible way, of course, but all the politeness and formality in the world couldn't cover the fact that he thought his wife superior to me.

I couldn't disagree. Alexis had great big blue doll eyes, and I

4

had dull green eyes reminiscent of an alley cat's. She had an ample bosom, and I had … well, never you mind. Basically, where Alexis was a short, blonde package of dynamite, I was more of a lanky brunette firecracker. And even that was pushing the envelope a bit.

Or a lot. Hell, I was probably best compared to a sparkler. You know, kind of exciting and something that your parents would approve of, or exactly the kind of awful person that could drive a fraction of the town insane with my inability to accept change, which in the vampire's minds meant zip codes.

I sipped my coffee and settled on the couch, offering her the other end. "Well, since you don't sleep, which I don't believe for a second, then you know all about the happenings in my front yard last night."

"Sure do," she said, taking the seat I indicated. "I did a drive-by to make sure they weren't killing anything … other than the flowers in your flowerbeds."

I darted out of my seat and peered out the living room window. "Okay, you can step all over the narcissus and stomp all the roses down, but you do not deflate the giant Santa Claus!" I sat back down and shook my head. "Madness … this is just madness."

She patted my shoulder. "Don't worry, Sapphire. The roses will grow back, and as far as Santa goes, you should have gotten a new one years ago. He's missing an arm. How did you even get him inflated?"

"Duct tape, but it won't do any good to get another one if they keep up the protests."

"Funny you should say that."

I tore my eyes from the rim of my mug. I knew that tone. That was the, 'There's something terrible happening that you're not going to like' tone. "Oh, for heaven's sake. What is it now?"

"You, my dear Sapphire, have a delightful, new vampire neighbor."

"You're kidding?" The townhouse next door was the only vacant space in Everlast. In fact, there was a waiting list a mile long for any other house, except the one next to mine. No one wanted to move to an all-inclusive vampire community, just to live next door to another human. Until now.

"Nope, not kidding. Sorry."

"Well? Who is he? She? They?"

"No clue. Ronan said that they weren't at all particular about who leased the house as long as a vampire did it. I don't think he went through the same screening process as everyone else."

"So, he could be a serial killer, or a rapist, or something?"

"With all the trouble you're causing in this town, you can pretty much guarantee he is … something."

"What?" I screeched.

"Relax, Sapphire. I'm kidding. You know Kinane won't let an undesirable in."

"That's true." King Kinane, as I liked to call him in private, had told me on the several occasions that he tried to 'talk some sense into me' that he longed for a perfect society. There was no way a smart and powerful man like that would put his brainchild at risk. He would hire a hit man to kill me first.

"And anyway, you're missing the point," she continued. "You know how vain vampires can be. No one is going to want to be seen carrying a picket sign through your yard. They'll want to be introduced in their best light. I doubt they'll be any protests for a while."

"You're right." I sighed, not looking forward to the prospect of a new problem taking the place of my old problem. "You know, for someone married to a bloodsucker, you're surprisingly harsh on their race."

"That's because they're surprisingly harsh on my race." She

6

stood to her feet and pulled me toward the bedroom. "Now, come on. That mail isn't going to stamp and sort itself."

Boy, was she ever right about that. I was only one of three humans willing to work for the Everlast post office. For me, it was no big deal. I'd worked there ever since it was the Peach post office. For the other two workers, it was just a place to work until their transfers finally came through. I couldn't seem to make them realize that if we go to work after the sun rises and clock out before the sun sets, there isn't any danger to be had from our pointy-toothed friends, but they would not be swayed. It was their loss. I loved the solitude of the daytime. It felt like it was my own little town when no one was awake. I often spent my lunch break sprawled underneath an oak tree in the park reading ... or sleeping. If Kieran only knew I did that right in front of his office, he would probably lose his mind. I bet he hated the thought of me roaming around in his town unsupervised. Probably as much as I loved the thought of him hating it.

***

With a promise to join her and Ronan for drinks the next evening, Alexis dropped me off in the parking lot at precisely nine o'clock and sped away, leaving me to my mundane existence. Some days, I really envied her easy life of privilege, until I remembered the boring monotony she endured every day. How many massage and hair appointments could you keep before you went insane? Thirty? Forty? Even I could see what an escape from reality it was here.

Sure, the clientele could be friendlier and/or easier to deal with, but they weren't the kind of people I was looking for approval from anyhow. Most were vampire pets, usually pale, gaunt imitations of their once healthy selves outfitted in black leather and ten or twenty piercings. They wandered in looking smug and self-important as they mailed off Visa bills and party invitations for their masters. Impressed, I was not. Ten to one, these 'pets' aren't the ones the vampires are using the Visas on or the ones getting invited to the luxurious, formal affairs that Alexis had told me so much about.

The morning went on as usual with nothing more exciting than running out of the medium-sized mailboxes and a misrouted package that should have gone to Phoenix. All in all, a good day, until a jumpy human came in with a change of address form to turn in for my new neighbor. I looked over the trembling young man for obvious signs of abuse or noticeable bites. He looked ... healthy. His rosy complexion perfectly complimented the dark hair above his chocolate brown eyes. Nope, there was nothing wrong with him that time wouldn't fix. He was just scared out of his wits. I had the same freaked out expression for the first three weeks the vampires started moving into town. If I were a betting woman, I would bet that today was the poor guy's first day on the job.

Smiling warmly, I handed him some helpful pamphlets for the new tenant and asked, "First day?"

He breathed out a shaky sigh. "That obvious, huh?"

"Well, you are over there fidgeting like you need your next fix," I said. He laughed, but it sounded forced to my ears. "Are you okay?"

Beckoning me closer, he leaned in to speak in hushed tones. "Can I ask you something?"

"Okay, shoot."

"How do you do it? How do you live here knowing that they don't want you? And how the Sam Hill do you get over the fear of them bleeding you dry?"

Great, my reputation had preceded me. "Oh. Is that all?" I waved off his hysteria with a hand. "That's easy. I don't think about it. If I did, I'd be shaking worse than you are now. You'll get used to them, and all this will seem really normal after a while."

"Well, it can be that way without me," he said. "I can't do this.

And to tell you the truth, I think they gave me this weirdo because I'm the new guy."

I raised my eyebrows. "Weirdo, huh? Yeah, they definitely saw you coming."

He threw the pamphlets back at me. "Well, tell them you saw me going, will ya?"

"O-okay."

I watched him stalk away with my mouth hanging open. Did I just talk him into quitting his job? Why couldn't I keep my big mouth shut? Oh, yeah. Two words—I'm nosy.

And to prove that beyond the shadow of a doubt, I spent the ten to eleven hour looking for dirt on the weirdo. I didn't have much success with my own Google searches, but with the limited postal resources at my disposal, I was able to discern that his name was Tobias Lukas Faust, and his last known address was in New Brunswick, Canada, by way of some town I couldn't pronounce in Germany. A German vampire! I wondered if he'd have an accent and a garden gnome in the front yard when I showed up on his doorstep tonight.

In Peach, there was only one way to find out who the new neighbor was, the old-fashioned way ... by showing up with the traditional Peach welcome casserole, or, in this case, a nice bottle of casserole. What was the worst that could happen? He could eat me? If I let that worry stop me, I wouldn't get anything done in this town. Plus, my Me-Maw would have approved of me being neighborly. She always did chide me for not visiting with the neighbors more often. I just didn't have the heart to tell her that sitting around eating cookies with seventy-year-old ladies wasn't my idea of a pleasant afternoon. Being a seventy-year-old lady with a fondness for Snickerdoodles, she probably wouldn't have appreciated that.

***

After work, I took the bus to the Target just out of town and splurged on a forty-four-dollar bottle of imported German blood, an extremely lucky find if I say so myself. Virginia wasn't exactly known for its fine imported blood selection or much else vampire related, for that matter. Actually, blood was hard to find on the shelf in most places, even big cities. Factor in the paranoid vampires that tend to stock up just in case the supply is tainted or just because they don't want to venture out for blood every week, and you have even less of a choice.

Thanks to the Greater Lynchburg Transit Company driver who noticed me running after him, I managed to make it home in record time to change out of my uniform. I wanted to look my best when I met Mr. Faust. Yes, I was still holding out hope that the neighbor would turn out to be hot, instead of a weirdo like his ex-assistant had mentioned. I wasn't scared to date vampires if they didn't turn out to be Dracula wannabes. Believe me. Those vampires were out there, and they were just as creepy as they sounded.

***

Once I got home and was groomed to relative perfection, I gathered all the courage I could muster and said, "You can do this, Sapphire," to the pale, scared woman in the hallway mirror then took the bottle and myself next door to face the new neighbor.

After a quick glance around the yard for gnomes, I tentatively knocked on the front door of Mr. Faust's huge, cookie-cutter townhouse and held my breath as I waited.

Thankfully, he didn't keep me waiting long. Following only a few moments of silence, I heard a deep, accented voice say, "Where the hell have you been?" and then the door swung open with an almost palpable urgency. I blinked up wordlessly at the man until he realized who he towered above.

"Pardon my language, Madam. How may I assist you this evening?"

At this point, I might have squeaked in response. It was hard to tell. My brain seemed to shut down when he smiled at me. It literally took my breath away, or maybe it was the rest of him that did it. Perfectly blended hair of blonde and brown, striking blue-green eyes, chiseled cover model features … yep, he was gorgeous, and I was way, way past desperate for male companionship. The world would truly be a cruel place if he turned out to be anything less than my knight in shining armor.

Tamping down my inner sex kitten, I gave him a winning smile of my own, crossing my fingers that he didn't notice my star-struck reaction. "I'm Sapphire Dragulj, from next door." I gestured to the ridiculously out of place two-story to my right. "I brought you a welcome to the neighborhood gift."

"Have you really?" he asked in wonder. "How very … neighborly. I am Tobias Faust." He paused and smiled again. "But, you probably already knew that from the change of address form, didn't you? You work at the post office if I understand it correctly from all your many … admirers."

Oh, great, my reputation preceded me again. I nodded in the affirmative, trying not to blush. "Guilty."

"Please, come in, and forgive the mess. I haven't had time to put everything away just yet."

He took the beaded, decorative wine bag I offered and welcomed me into the foyer, managing to help me take off my coat and hang it on the rack with his free hand.

"Impressive dexterity, there. Thanks."

"I do what I can," he said, grinning as he led me into his gleaming, immaculate kitchen. "I must admit that I am surprised by your arrival. I wasn't expecting a warm, cordial gesture from you. Not after the town's repeated warnings about your anti-vampire stance." He tsked me teasingly. "Superiority is not a very becoming trait in a human, you know."

I appreciated him making light of the situation, but holy shit was I pissed at whoever told him that lie. Of all the nerve! The vampires around here couldn't wait to throw me out on my ass, and then they turn around and make me out to be the racist one? Well, doesn't that just figure?

Pinching the bridge of his nose, he shook his head. "I can see that the American vampires have made the same impression upon humans as the German and Canadian ones have since our coming out. Allow me to apologize for my race. They can be a little …."

"Self-entitled? Pushy?" I suggested, huffing in frustration.

"Oh, yes, and several other adjectives. Some that aren't polite to say in good society. They really do hate you here, don't they?"

"Not everyone, but I'm pretty sure that most don't think I'm good enough to be on their planet, much less their neighborhood, although I like to believe that has more to do with my house than my being a human."

He laughed and motioned for me to take a seat at the bar. "I think you're holding on to false hope there. I moved in while they held their protest in the middle of your flower garden. What do we want? No humans! When do we want it? Now!" he mocked. "Originality isn't this town's strong suit, is it?"

Heat filled my cheeks. How embarrassing! "No, I'm afraid not," I said, sighing. "I hate that you had to go through that on your first night here. Wait a minute." I looked around me, carefully this time. Everything, and I mean everything, looked to be in its proper place. No boxes stacked up, no drinking out of the sugar bowl because he couldn't find the box with the glasses—nothing. It was incredibly put together for just one night's work. "Did you say that you moved in last night?"

"Super speed is one of the greatest gifts us superior vampire gods have. I wouldn't expect a lowly human to understand."

"Funny," I grouched.

"Exceedingly," he said with a wink. "Now, what kind of wine did you bring?" He had the blood bottle out of the bag and was reading the label before I could tell him it wasn't wine. "You …

you brought me blood?"

"Well, yeah. My grandmother would skin me alive if she knew I didn't welcome a new neighbor with a casserole, or a peach cobbler, or something. And since you don't eat …" I drifted off, lifting my eyebrows.

Watching him closely for his reaction, I could pinpoint the exact moment he lost control. His eyes grew amber with hunger, and the bottle began to tremble in his hands. He needed to feed, badly. That explained the urgency when he opened the door.

"I, uh … I need to leave," he said, thrusting his hand into his pocket and jerking out his house keys. He dropped them on the counter. "See yourself out, will you?"

"Where…" I started, but the screen door was already slamming behind him.

Surprised, I stared at the place he had stood for another moment then sprang into action. I didn't feel comfortable being in his house alone. Placing the bottle into a fancy modern wine rack, I jogged to the door, dropping the keys into the mailbox on the way out. I was starting to understand why the man had said he was a weirdo this morning. New or not, that guy picked up on it right away. My neighbor, Tobias, was a vampire that struggled against his true nature.

CHAPTER TWO

The next morning, I woke up to Marvin Gaye's, I Want You, blaring from my cell phone. There could only be one person calling me at sunup on a Saturday. Alexis delighted in knowing I never kept my phone in the bedroom and would have to go downstairs in order to answer it. She was evil, I tell you … just plain evil. Nice, decent people let their friends sleep in on their weekends off.

After a few minutes of refusing to get up, I caved and dragged myself out of bed to dial my voicemail. I sighed wearily as Alexis' animated voice came blaring through the speaker at a volume that would never be appropriate at the crack of dawn.

"HEY, SAPH! COME TO OUR HOUSE AT DARK. RONAN SAW KIERAN AND THE NEW GUY LAST NIGHT. I KNOW EVERYTHING ABOUT YOUR NEW NEIGHBOR!"

Well, of course, she knew. She probably had a Mrs. Bennet moment and badgered Ronan until he went to see Kiernan to set up a meeting with Tobias. I pressed seven to erase her message and went to the next one. It was her again. This time she spoke in a sing-song voice.

"CHECK YOUR PORCH, GIRLIE! SOMEONE LEFT YOU ROSES!"

I dropped the phone and ran, snatching my coat from the back of a chair and wriggling into it as I rushed to open the front door. Sure enough, there sat at least three dozen red roses in a magnificent crystal vase. I couldn't imagine who would have sent me these. Looking around the deserted neighborhood, I didn't see an immediate explanation, so I carefully picked up the massive arrangement and took it inside to look for a card. After a few seconds of panicked searching, I found a small black envelope from the all-night florist—not a surprise, since there's only one in town.

ALL I WANT FOR CHRISTMAS ARE MY TWO FRONT FANGS

Carefully opening the delicate stationery, I tugged the note out. Scrawled in untidy handwriting, it read simply,

Thanks for your kindness.

T

The T stood for Tobias. It had to. No other vampire in town would send me flowers.

Smiling like a loon, I took the display to the dining room and sat them in front of the unadorned window facing his house. I wanted him to see how beautiful the flowers looked on my grandmother's credenza when he woke from his death sleep.

Why did I want him to see them? I hadn't quite figured that out yet. I mean, of course, I thought Tobias was attractive. Most male vampires were uncommonly handsome. However, his reaction to a still stoppered bottle of blood troubled me. It would be stupid to put myself in unnecessary danger just to try to snag a husband. I wasn't that desperate—yet.

***

Alexis' high spirits, or should I say, high consumption of spirits, was evident as I walked up her artfully landscaped driveway. She let out a squeal and snatched the storm door open to tug me into a tight hug. "Hey, girl! I just tried to call your house. Ronan would have picked you up. You know I hate it when you walk at night."

"Alex, they're people just like us. Nothing is going to happen to me on the one block walk from my house to here. A vampire attacking me on the street would be like me chasing around a cow with a knife and fork." I shook my head. "You watch too many movies."

"Maybe you don't watch enough," Ronan argued, planting a

protective, brotherly kiss on my forehead. "You can never be too careful."

"Yeah, yeah. Thanks, Grandpa. So," I prompted. "What's the deal on Tobias Faust?"

"Oh no," Alexis interjected. "She has to be adequately tipsy before I tell her what you found out, Ronan."

"As you wish, my love. Though, I wasn't going to tell her anything about her criminal neighbor after that Grandpa remark. That never gets any funnier, Sapphire."

"Criminal? Oh, Lord." Well, there went that vampire lover fantasy. It probably wouldn't have worked out anyway. Unless it's in an opaque bottle, I faint at the sight of blood.

"We'll have time to pray later," Alexis teased, laughing at my dramatics. "Come on, I bought that expensive French champagne you love."

"Of course, you did, Princess. Your perfect life makes mine seem so depressing. You're like a walking faerytale."

"Hey, don't hate because I got my happily ever after. You'll find yours. We just need to concentrate on finding your prince."

"Awesome. Why didn't I think of doing that?" I deadpanned, watching her walk up the steps and into the house. "Ronan, can't you get her a dog to lavish her attention on or something?"

"She's your best friend, lass. You knew what you were getting into."

"Ugh. You know how I feel about that leprechaun talk." He only pulled out the big guns when he wanted to sway me.

Ronan flashed his fangs and growled, "Do I look like a leprechaun to you?"

Sighing heavily, I looked at his perfectly styled black hair and eyes and shook my head. "No. You look like every hero, slash, good guy in every faerytale, rolled into one."

"Yes, and you look like the cute and quirky best friend. We all have our parts to play in Alexis' 'perfect life', you know."

The slightly manic gleam in his dark eyes as he spoke unnerved me. I squinted at him, examining his face. "She's driving you crazy, isn't she? That's why she's so gung-ho on setting me up. You're putting her up to it!"

"Shhhhhhh," he hissed, casting a furtive glance at the house. "Sapphire, you have no idea what it's like! She needs a hobby. Please, before I lose my mind."

Of all the sneaky, conniving a-holes! He knew I couldn't turn down that puppy dog face. Oh, but he would pay for this crime against humanity. Alexis on a mission was a thing to behold. Just ask the entire staff of Neiman Marcus. We're both banned from the store for the scene she caused over a Prada bag in May. I'll never be able to look at mannequins the same.

"Fine. I'll be Alexis' Barbie, but just so you know, I think it's a lost cause. Not many vampires in this town will agree to date me."

He put his arm around my shoulders and led me up the stairs to the front door. "Thank you. Your magnanimous gesture will live on forever in this cold, dead heart of mine. And, just so you know, you'd be surprised just how wrong you are about finding a suitor. I happen to know at least one vampire likes you enough to send flowers at Tricia's exorbitant prices."

"Yes, and he has excellent taste," Alexis added, handing me a champagne flute.

I sighed again. "Too bad he's a criminal. He's kind of the whole package, funny and handsome with that great accent."

"Whole package or not, murder eliminates him from the running," Ronan insisted.

Alexis shook her blonde curls. "No, it doesn't."

"Yes, it does!" Ronan and I screeched in unison. There was no way that I was going to date a vampire that lacked control of his bloodlust.

"Don't be ridiculous, you two! What vampire hasn't had some kind of incident? Show me one."

I scooted out from under Ronan's arm. "I'm guessing Ronan isn't the one?"

"No, he's lost control plenty of times. He never really hurts me when he attacks."

"Sapphire don't listen to her," Ronan warned, looking mortified. "It's dangerous."

"Oh, come on. It happens. It's in your nature. Nothing could be so sexy or primal. To be honest, it makes me hot just thinking about it. The sex, Sapphire, the sex!"

"Okay, okay. I get it. The sex, it's sexy. Can I ask how long you've been drinking?"

"Since one o'clock? Don't you get on my case about it, too! Ronan's been lecturing me since he got up. It's been a hard day, okay?"

"My love, I just worry that something will happen when I cannot help you," Ronan told her.

She snuggled into her husband's chest. "I won't have to worry about that for long, will I?"

He wrapped his arms around her, holding her tightly. "No, a stóirín. Soon, you will be mine forever."

Ah, now the early afternoon drinking made sense. Alexis was going to go through with the change. "When is it?" I asked, bracing myself. I knew this day would happen. Ronan had been trying to convince her to be made vampire since their marriage. Her being a human was a constant concern for him. She was so fragile, so breakable—so mortal.

"Soon," they answered together.

ALL I WANT FOR CHRISTMAS ARE MY TWO FRONT FANGS

I sighed and threw back the glass of champagne. "Where's the bottle, Alexis? I'm going to need it if my only human friend is going to the dark side."

***

Three episodes of True Blood later, I sat pleasantly drunk and tucked into Ronan's Mercedes for the thirty-second trip home. He insisted that he take me, and I didn't stop him. Not only did I think I might fall into Mr. Lunsford's azaleas, but after Ronan's tale of horror, starring the one and only Tobias Faust, I didn't want to be alone in the night with him living so close. I fully expected to have nightmares of him chasing me with a knife and fork tonight.

"So, to recap, Sapphire. No walking at night. No more visits to see the man next door, no matter how … hot, and pepper spray is always on your person, right?"

I patted my pocket. "Right here, Ronan. And don't worry, I won't be going anywhere near him or any other vampires at night after hearing that story. I still can't believe he got away with killing those tourists in Germany."

"Believe it," he said, slowing down to a crawl and carefully turning his car around in the cul-de-sac to pull up to the curb in front of my house. "Promise me that you won't put yourself in danger."

"I've been living with vampires for two years, some of them repeat offenders when it comes to losing control of their bloodlust, and I've never had a problem. Why is there this sudden urgency for my safety? It's kind of freaking me out."

"I'm about to go one step past freaking you out," he assured me, taking my hand and pressing a small vial into my palm. "I don't know how you feel about becoming one of us. I didn't want to pry. But now that you've got danger so close to your home, I'm begging you to hold on to this. If you are hurt, drink it. You will only go through the change if you have a fatal injury."

I stared at the nauseating little bottle. "Gross, Ronan."

"You'll thank me when your throat is ripped out, and you're dying in the gutter, lass."

I narrowed my eyes at him.

"Please," he pleaded, switching tactics. "Alexis will never recover if anything ever happened to you."

"Okay, seriously, you're ten seconds from checking the closet, under the bed, and the perimeter of the yard for monsters."

"That, I will gladly do. Actually, that makes me feel a little better about leaving you here." He hesitated, mulling over his words. "Sapphire, pride aside, are you sure you wouldn't rather move in with us? Even if it's only until this whole protest/new neighbor thing blows over?"

I kissed him on the cheek. "Thanks for the offer, Ronan, really, but if I ever do move in with a vampire, it will be with one of my own." I stepped out onto the sidewalk and ducked my head back in. "See you soon, and uh…" I tucked the vial into my pocket. "Thanks for everything."

His black eyes twinkled in the streetlight. "Of course, love. Now get yourself inside."

Stumbling through the trampled garden, I climbed the stairs to my front door and waved. He returned the motion and drove away slowly, no doubt making sure I got in okay.

"Hallo, Saphir," A deep voice said from behind me.

Like any self-respecting feminist, I promptly dropped my keys and screamed like a little girl as I spun around to find Tobias standing there, a broad smile stretched across his face. "I apologize. I didn't mean to alarm you."

"That's okay," I wheezed out, holding my heart and laughing at my ridiculousness. "I'm just a little jumpy. It's dark, and you know…" I looked around the empty street, and mock whispered, "Vampires."

ALL I WANT FOR CHRISTMAS ARE MY TWO FRONT FANGS

"Loathsome creatures, those."

"The loathsome-ist," I agreed, trembling slightly as I picked up my keys. "So, what brings you by?"

Please, please, please don't say to eat me.

"Plum cake," he answered, pulling a covered pie plate from out of nowhere.

"You bought me a cake?"

"Nein, engel. I baked you a cake."

"You bake?"

He shrugged. "I have little to occupy my time."

"Oh." Well, of course, the hot, foreign vampire next door baked. It was just my luck that he would turn out to be perfect in every way but the homicidal way. What did I do in a past life to deserve this kind of bad luck? Could nothing ever be simple?

He smiled fondly at me. "It was nothing, really."

Oh, no. Hot, foreign guy did not just smile at me like that. I knew that smile. Granted, I hadn't seen it in a couple years, but that was an unmistakable 'I like you' smile.

"It's just too bad you went to all the trouble, and you can't eat any of it," I said eager to fill the silence.

"It is a shame. It was once my favorite. However, I can watch you eat it ... if you invite me in," he hinted, calling me out on my rudeness. He invited me into his home when I was a stranger, after all, and here I was making him stand on the porch when he held yet another gift in his hands.

Ignoring the unbearable decibel of the warning bells going off in my stupid, drunken brain, I let the politeness that my grandmother had insisted on make my decision for me and unlocked the door. "I'm so sorry. How rude of me. Come inside and make yourself at home."

"Thank you." He stepped past me with a wink, making me shiver down to my toes. Shit. I was in so much trouble.

"Can I get you something to drink?" I asked, taking the pie from him to put it on the kitchen counter. "I've got wine, coffee, bl—"

"Red wine, if you have it," he interrupted, saving us from an uncomfortable repeat of last night. "Saphir, I must apologize for my behavior. It is inexcusable."

"It's fine," I assured him, pretending to be absorbed in opening a bottle of Bordeaux. "It happens from time to time, right? It just wasn't the most opportune time, that's all."

"You're being kind."

"Yes. But what would you have me do? Yell at you? Berate you for being yourself?" I handed him his glass. "How can I when you're so obviously sorry for what you did? You sent me flowers and baked me a cake, for Pete's sake."

He caught my hand as I came around the counter with my own glass. "I would do more to have you forget that it happened at all."

His touch felt electric, pulsating wildly through me. It was as if he caressed my whole body, instead of just taking my hand. I blew out a shaky breath. "Tobias, I need to sit down."

In seconds, he had a chair pulled out and was easing me into it. "What can I do to help you? You are very pale."

"I'm okay, really. I drank a bottle of champagne on an empty stomach at my friend's house tonight. It seemed like such a good idea at the time."

He pressed a cool hand to my forehead. "It usually does. Shall I put you to bed, or perhaps, you'd feel better after a slice of cake?"

"A slice of cake would be great. The plates are in the cabinet over the counter, and the silverware is in the um...."

ALL I WANT FOR CHRISTMAS ARE MY TWO FRONT FANGS

Damn it. Where did I keep the silverware?

"The kitchen? Yes, that is where it is normally kept," he teased. "I'll be right back."

True to his word, he returned before I could finish my internal reprimand for this monumentally bad idea. I was probably going to be dead before midnight because I was a sucker for flowers and baked goods. Ronan had been downright prophetic to give me the vial of his blood. He could probably sense that I was the kind of pathetic person that would need it twenty minutes after I got it.

"So, tell me," Tobias asked, taking the adjacent chair and pushing a perfectly cut slice of deliciousness toward me. "Who is your friend?"

"Alexis—she's Ronan's wife. I heard you met him already."

"Yes, the Irish fellow—your lover."

I nearly choked on the forkful of cake in my mouth. "No!" I sputtered. "Why would you say that? He and I have only ever been friends."

"Does he know that? He nearly bit my head off when I mentioned our meeting last night. And the kiss you shared in the car, it didn't look innocent to me. At least, not on his end. I believe he may be a little enamored with you."

"Ronan is like a brother to me, and he feels the same. As a matter of fact, he begged me to let Alexis find a man for me tonight. She tends to drive him crazy when she doesn't have a project to work on."

Cupping my cheek, he asked, "And you are her next project?"

"Y-yes," I stammered, leaning into his hand and closing my eyes as he traced his cool fingers along my jaw.

"How does one apply for this project?" he asked, replacing his fingers with soft kisses.

"You …" I trailed off as he moved his mouth over mine, lost

in the tender way he barely brushed against my lips with feather-light kisses … just a whisper of the passion I knew he restrained within him. Restrained or not, it still made my brain fuzzy.

Groaning, I pushed myself away from him. How did I let it get this far already? I was a reasonably intelligent girl. I should be able to control my lust until I find out whether he intends to murder me, right? "Sorry, Tobias, just let me catch my breath, okay?"

Tobias' expression held an alarming amount of remorse for someone who had just knocked the socks off of an unsuspecting woman using only his lips. "It's me that's sorry, Saphir. I seem to keep overstepping boundaries with you."

The sharp peal of the doorbell made us both jump. "Who can that be at this time of night?" I wondered aloud.

Tobias took a deep breath, scenting the air. "It is your admirer—the Irishman," he whispered, not wanting to be overheard. "Shall I slip out the back door?"

"No! And he's not an admirer!" I hissed. "If you saw his gorgeous wife, you'd know how silly that sounds. Also, can I tell you how crazy it is that you can smell him all the way from here? That is truly bizarre."

"Be that as it may," Tobias pressed. "He knows I'm here, and his anger is evident." He tapped his nose. "The smell of jealousy is an acrid, unmistakable scent."

I didn't have time to wonder how he knew that. Ronan had stopped ringing the bell in favor of insistently pounding on the door and yelling out my name. Hurrying over, I quickly opened the door to find a slightly disheveled version of the vampire I knew standing on my doorstep.

Tobias put a protective hand on my shoulder. "Hallo, Ronan."

His eyes widened at Tobias' close proximity. "What is he doing here, Sapphire?"

"He brought me cake," I answered, sheepishly holding up the

fork that was somehow still in my hand. I knew from experience that the stern look on Ronan's face meant I was about to get the tongue lashing of my life.

"And now you're leaving?" Ronan asked, addressing the vampire standing behind me like a German guard dog.

"I am," Tobias grunted through gritted teeth, sounding none too pleased with Ronan's aggressive tone. "Saphir, it has been a great pleasure spending time with you. I hope to have the privilege much more often."

I stood on my toes to kiss his cheek. I didn't intend on letting Ronan push me around in my own house, regardless of his good intentions. "Thank you. You know where I live if you need to borrow a cup of sugar."

He brought my hand to his cold lips. "Are you saying that you approve of my baking prowess?"

Was he kidding? I approved of all the prowess he had, and I would be recounting every one of them when I was alone and under the covers later tonight. "I approve," I told him, trying not to blush.

"Until then, Saphir." He nodded at Ronan. "Seward."

Ronan returned the curt goodbye. "Faust."

"Good night, both of you." I sighed, exasperated at their show of testosterone, then moved to close the door. Ronan stopped me.

"A moment, Sapphire?"

I rolled my eyes. I knew what this would entail. "What is it?"

He stepped in and closed the door. "Are you out of your fucking senses? Did you not listen to a word I said out there? He's a murderer!"

"I'm sorry! I'm drunk. I had a moment of weakness."

"That moment could have cost you your life, Sapphire. Is that what you want—to die at the hands of a vampire?"

And there it was—the moment of truth. "Yes, Ronan, I do, if I'm being a hundred percent honest with myself. Of course, I want to be like you, like everyone in this town. And why shouldn't I? You're beautiful, strong, and gifted in every conceivable way. No, there's no question. If I find a man that loves me enough to spend an eternity with me, I would do it in a heartbeat."

The angry furrow between Ronan's dark brows softened. "It is not a life for you, Sapphire. I would only choose it if there were no other alternative."

"Let me understand this," I slurred, unconsciously brandishing the fork like a weapon. "It's good enough for your wife, but not for me? What? Am I not pretty enough to get in your super-secret club?"

He closed his hand over the business end of the fork, gently tugged it from my grasp, and set it on an end table. "Sapphire, you are one of the most classically beautiful women I've ever met. Your beauty isn't the problem. It's your spirit. I can't imagine a greater waste than you giving up your life to become a slave to the night."

I crossed my arms. "Bullshit."

He seized my shoulders and gave me a little shake. "You are willfully misunderstanding me! I said once that you two are opposites. Even in this circumstance, you can see that. Look at her, Sapphire. She can't make it on her own in this world. You can. You can live, have a husband, children, a house in the suburbs— anything you desire. You don't have to limit yourself like this. You're stronger than we are."

Did he just call himself weak? "I don't know what to say, Ronan."

He opened the door and looked back at me. "Don't say anything. Just think about what I said, and for the love of God, stay away from the murderer next door. I can't believe how many times I've had to say that to you tonight."

ALL I WANT FOR CHRISTMAS ARE MY TWO FRONT FANGS

"Yes, sir," I said, saluting.

He sighed and shut the door without another word.

CHAPTER THREE

Not about to let sanity deter me from my mission of doom, I watched Ronan's car until his taillights faded into the dark then ran upstairs to the window overlooking Tobias' side yard. There he stood, barefoot, his shirtless chest lit by the full moon. I couldn't believe someone so gorgeous could be interested in me, murderer or not. What could he see in me that no one else could? My common sense was screaming at me that it was my blood, but somehow, I couldn't force myself to believe that, or maybe, I just didn't want to.

I knocked on the window to get Tobias' attention and waved. He smiled up, pointed in the direction of my driveway, and held up a 'what gives' motion. I shrugged and fogged up the glass with my breath, writing my number backward, hoping he could read it from this distance. He held up a finger, jogging into the house, and a minute later, the phone rang.

Channeling my thirteen-year-old self, I flopped on the bed to grab my phone off the nightstand. *"Hi, Tobias."*

"Hallo, engel."

"I'm really sorry about all that weirdness with Ronan. I'm afraid he's taking his brotherly protective role a little too seriously."

"He cares for you, Saphir. That much is plain to see. As is the frightening intensity of his jealousy. Is he to be your maker?"

"No," I answered, deciding not to mention the vial of blood in my pocket. *"I'm not scheduled to become a vampire anytime soon."*

"I feel certain the Irishman will make you an offer of immortality. His attachment to you is a strong one if he is that interested in your safety."

ALL I WANT FOR CHRISTMAS ARE MY TWO FRONT FANGS

"You know," I ventured, knowing that it was a terrible idea before it came out of my mouth. *"We could be having this conversation in person. Ronan's long gone."*

"There is nothing I would rather do more." He paused as if choosing his words carefully. *"But I do not think this is the last time Ronan will visit you tonight. It's better if he doesn't sense me there."*

"You're right. He'll probably make another drive by. Like I said, he treats me as he would a sister."

"An obsessed brother." He chuckled darkly. *"I believe I can hear his car coming down the street again."*

Jumping up from the bed, I edged to the window and peeked out. Sure enough, Ronan was approaching the house at a crawl. I ducked my head back and sat down on the bed. *"You called it."*

"Shhhhh…" he whispered, then he was silent for several long moments. *"He's gone. Come to your back door."*

Giddy with the excitement of a long-awaited romance, I ran down the stairs two and a time and quickly unlatched and opened the old-fashioned door. I found my gorgeous, foreign suitor waiting there, a sexy smile perched on his full lips.

"Hi," I said.

He inclined his head. *"Guten abend, Saphir."*

We stood silent, staring at one another for a moment. "Do you plan on moving past the doorstep?" I asked, trying to break the ice.

"I definitely want to," he said. "I'm just not sure I should. It could be a bad idea."

"Why would it be a bad idea?"

Tobias leveled his blue-green gaze at me. "I am not always in control of my … urges."

I thought back to what Alexis had said earlier. "So, what you're telling me is that you're a vampire?"

The corners of his mouth twitched up. "Precisely."

I shrugged. "I think we can risk it."

He stepped closer to cup my face. "I hope I don't disappoint you, engel."

My brain ceased all function when his lips touched mine. This kiss was different than earlier. Ravenous and hungry, there was an urgency to his movements like he craved my mouth, needed it to survive. Something clicked into place in my fuzzy head.

Wait a minute. He craved me? He was ravenously hungry? Shit. What was I doing?

Pushing against his firm chest, I broke the best … and worst kiss of my life. "Hold on," I panted. I looked around. How did I get on top of the counter?

"Are you well?" he asked, looking concerned.

"Maybe we should take it a little slower," I answered, trying not to look at his eyes. "I don't want our first time to be on the kitchen counter."

Fangs extended, he grinned. "Are you so sure that we will know each other in that way?"

I looked from his fangs to the sizable bulge pressed against me. "Yep."

His brows lifted. "I look forward to it. How's tomorrow for you?"

I laughed. "I'll check with Alexis to see if Ronan will be playing chaperone, and I'll let you know."

He rested his forehead against my shoulder. "Saphir, your heart beats so fast. If you're frightened of me, do not hesitate to speak up. I abhor the thought of scaring you."

"I'm sorry," I said, extremely aware that his fangs were in close proximity to my neck.

"There's no need to apologize," he told me, waving away my apology. "I was once a human. I remember fear and worry well."

"You were made?" I asked. "The rumor going around is that you were born a vampire."

He stroked my cheek. "Tomorrow, I shall tell you all. Will you come to me at dusk?"

"Yes, but are you sure I should meet you at your house? I mean, do you really want the neighborhood to see their most hated enemy at your door twice in one week?"

I think we can risk it," he said with a wink.

"Good."

"Tomorrow," he growled, before capturing my bottom lip between his teeth and kissing me until I was breathless.

I staggered a little when he pulled away. "Wow."

He grinned devilishly. *"Gute nacht, Saphir."*

Mouth agape and swollen, I stared as he closed the back door behind him. Like an idiot, I couldn't wait until tomorrow.

***

I woke in the early afternoon, still feeling a little woozy. The jury was out on whether it was the alcohol or the sexy vampire neighbor that caused it. Last night had been … interesting. To say the least, Tobias had surprised me. Mainly, with his marked romantic interest. What could he want with someone so normal, so decidedly plain … someone like me? I didn't have extraordinary beauty like Alexis or wealth like some of the female vampires in town. Really, I had nothing to offer Tobias—except blood, perhaps. I didn't want to think about it.

Instead, I went about my usual Sunday routine. I made coffee, thought about cleaning, decided not to, showered, and then went to check my Facebook page. If anything, I was a creature of habit.

As soon as I logged on, I found Tobias had sent me a friend

request. Weird. Okay, maybe not that weird. I knew vampires lived just as humans do, but it was still a little hard to imagine a blood-drinking creature of the night chatting on Facebook. I accepted his request and immediately started stalking … I mean, looking at his page. He had an album of the city lights of Toronto and Munich and a few check-ins at restaurants and bars in both Canada and the United States. That was about it. It was really … normal. I went back to his home page and read his last status.

Ich traf einen engel. Ich glaube, ich bin verliebt.

German, of course. Thank God for Google Translate. I opened up a new tab and copied and pasted the text. It translated to 'I met an angel. I think I'm in love'.

Holy. Shit. He thought he was in love? I repeat. Holy. Shit!

Grinning like a fool, I looked around for my cell. I needed Alexis here … now.

She answered on the first ring. *"I didn't think you'd be up after the amount of booze you had last night."*

"Me?" I scoffed. *"What about you? You said you'd been drinking since one o'clock!"*

"Whatever. What's up? Do you want to get lunch out of town? I'm craving pork dumplings."

"Yes! I have exciting news!" I sang.

"What? Tell me!"

"Not yet. Get here. Now."

I heard her Mercedes crank up. *"I'm already on my way."*

Alexis came through the door a minute later, still in her pajama bottoms. "Nice pants," I snarked.

"They cover my ass, right?" She flopped down on the couch face first. "Ugh. I feel like shit. Remind me never to drink again."

"Fine. I'll do it for you. I could use one right about now."

Alexis lifted her head. "Why? What's going on?"

I motioned toward next door. "Come over here, and be really quiet, okay."

Positively alarmed at my abnormal behavior, she sat in the office chair I held out and looked obediently at what I had to show her. "So, sexy-man Faust has a Facebook page. What's the big deal?"

I clicked over to the other tab. "Look what his last status translates to."

Wide-eyed, she looked at me. "And you think he's talking about you?"

"Well, yeah. I'm not a complete troll, am I?"

"Not completely," she said in a perfectly serious voice. "What am I missing here?"

"Just the fact that Tobias baked me a plum cake, made out with me on the kitchen counter, and asked me to come over tonight."

Her mouth dropped open. "What?"

"And he's nicknamed me angel!"

She narrowed her eyes. "Are you fucking with me?"

I held up three fingers. "Scout's honor."

"Forget lunch. You need a makeover."

"What? What do you mean?" Horrified, I ran to the mirror in the foyer and stared at the ponytail on top of my head and my sexy ensemble of sweatpants and a Peach High Cobblers (yes, cobblers) t-shirt. Damn, she was right. I hadn't had my hair professionally cut in over four years, and my clothes made me look like the world's youngest grandma. Honestly, I was surprised Tobias even gave me a second glance looking like this. I walked back to the living room, distraught by my findings. "Uh … Alexis?"

She smirked at my panicked expression. "Yeah?"

I fell to my knees. "Help me."

"I'll do what I can, but I'm no miracle worker." She grinned and ducked the throw pillow I aimed at her head. "But before I do anything, I need coffee … or I'm just going to pass right out."

***

After giving Alexis a cup filled to the brim with hazelnut flavored goodness, I sat quietly, pondering how far I was willing to go with this makeover thing. I needed something easy and manageable if I was going to make big changes. I didn't want the kind of makeup and hair that would take me two hours. This town already had one Alexis. And thirty minutes of maintenance was my hard limit. I wasn't into torture.

I was just about to tell her to call the whole thing off when there was a light knock at the door. Alexis looked at me from where she sat watching cartoons and shrugged. I shrugged back and heaved myself out of my grandpa's La-Z-Boy.

Foot traffic during the day in Everlast was practically nonexistent, and I hadn't ordered anything, so it was surprising to find a small, dark-haired woman on my doorstep. "Can I help you?" I asked, looking behind her. There was a tall, burly man in a suit leaning against the hood of a black stretch limo with windows so tinted, I couldn't see inside. He was either a chauffeur or a hitman.

"Are you, Saphir?" she asked.

There was only one person who would call me that—Tobias. "It's Sapphire in English, but yes, I'm Saphir."

She grinned. "Great! I'm Claire. I work in the boutique in the square downtown." My confused face spurred her to continue. "I'm guessing Mr. Faust didn't tell you that he came in to purchase a dress for you last night. He asked me to do what was necessary to find out your size."

34

"So, you've come down here in a limo to measure me?" I asked stupidly.

Claire giggled and shook her head. "I thought we might ride to the store where we keep the dresses, and you could try them on."

"I'm so sorry," I said, blushing bright red. "My brain isn't working yet. I kind of overdid it last night. Come on in, and make yourself at home while I find my purse. There's a fresh pitcher of tea in the fridge if you're interested."

"Really?" She beamed at me. "I can't remember the last time I was offered something to drink. Vampires seem to forget about the needs of humans, regardless of how many humans they have as pets and employees."

Wow. My manager may be surly, but at least she remembered that I get dehydrated easily.

"Have you ever thought about another line of work?" I asked.

"No way. I like it at the boutique. The vampire I work for lets me have the run of the place. And he supplies protection during the night. It's a pretty sweet gig."

"Hey, Claire. I thought I heard your voice," Alexis said, yawning as she joined us in the foyer. She handed me her empty coffee cup and put on her best Oliver Twist voice. "Please sir, I want some more."

I rolled my eyes. "You know where the kitchen is."

She scoffed. "I'm a guest!"

"You're a nuisance," I retorted.

Claire cleared her throat. "Ladies…"

"Can I just give you a blanket apology for everything you have and will witness today while you're in our company?" I asked.

"Accepted," she said with a wink.

"So, Claire, what are you doing here?" Alexis gasped. "Are you here to dress Miss I Have No Discernible Style? Please say you are."

"Well, as a matter of fact, I am. Tobias Faust commissioned my services for Miss Dragulj last night. I was going to call you after I finished. Your special order came in this morning."

"Awesome! I'll come by as soon as I can legally drive."

Claire looked from Alexis to me. "What did y'all get up to last night?"

"A boozy True Blood marathon," I told her.

"Ah. Well, you're both welcome to come back to the shop with me. Samuel will drive us."

"Can Samuel take us by Starbucks first?" Alexis asked, peering into her empty coffee cup.

"He better," Claire said. "I don't think she's going to make it without it. How much did you guys drink last night?"

"When did you start drinking is the question you want to ask her," I supplied, sidestepping Alexis' swat.

"Bite me, Sapphire."

"Isn't Ronan going to do that?" I teased. "I don't think I'd have much luck making you a vampire."

"Sapphire!" she yelled, giving me an angry stare. "I can't believe you outed me to Claire!"

Claire laughed. "I think I would have noticed when you started coming in at night. You're one of only three daytime customers."

"That's true," Alexis conceded. "So, what's with the limo?"

"Ask your friend. It's her beau that paid for it."

"What?" I asked, completely dumbfounded by the turn of events. I was going to need a paper bag to breathe into if Tobias kept this up. He was moving so fast!

ALL I WANT FOR CHRISTMAS ARE MY TWO FRONT
FANGS

Claire grinned and lowered her voice to a whisper. "Mr. Faust came in last night and looked at every dress at least ten times. There were two that I could tell he favored, but I think he wanted to let you choose what you like. Eventually, he gave me a two-thousand dollar down payment and asked me to rent a limo and let you have your pick of the dresses, panties, garters, bras—whatever you want. It was pretty cute, actually."

"Seriously?" Alexis asked. "I love Ronan and all, but does this guy have a brother?"

"I have no idea," I said. "We just met the night before last. I barely know him."

"So, flowers, cake, and now, a dress? What's next? A new car? I sure hope so," Alexis grumped. "I'm getting tired of hauling your ass around."

"What? You beg me to let you take me!"

She looked horrified. "I do, don't I?"

Claire shook her head. "You guys are so weird. Are you ready to go?"

I looked down at my sad clothes and smiled at the prospect of a new dress. "Very."

***

My first time in a limo was just as cool as I hoped it would be. Claire's driver, Samuel, told me to 'go crazy' as he held the door for me, and I did. He smiled at me in the rear-view mirror as I tried every button and laughed out loud when I excitedly found a bottle of champagne.

"I could get used to this," I declared, relaxing into the plush black leather seat for the two-minute drive. "Hey, Samuel, how many people say that when they get in here?"

He winked at me. "You're the first one."

"Thought so," I said, winking back. "So, Claire, tell us about the dresses Tobias favored." I took the champagne from Alexis when she picked it up. "None for you, Alex."

She collapsed back into the seat and took a long draw of her caramel macchiato. "Probably a good call."

"Just wait until you see them," Claire said, leaning forward to hold out her glass. "You're going to love them."

It turned out that Claire's words were one hundred percent true. As soon as she unlocked the door to let us in the shop, I made a beeline to one of the dresses Tobias had favored. It was red, low-cut, and body-hugging. I wasn't sure how I could pull it off, but I damn sure wanted to try. It was beautiful.

The other dress Claire showed me was even more risqué— short with a mixture of black lace and sheer fabric that left nothing to the imagination. "These are …" I struggled to finish my sentence.

"Amazing?" Alexis asked. "Seriously, they will both look gorgeous on you."

"I don't know."

Claire grabbed a red size six off the rack and handed it to me. "I do. Go put this on. You're going to look fantastic."

While I was extremely skeptical, I took the dress and went in the direction she pointed to. There was no way I would look halfway decent in this. I was too tall, too gangly, not nearly curvy enough.

"We want to see it," Claire called after me. "No trying it on and not showing us, okay?"

"Fine," I grumbled. "Prepare to be underwhelmed."

In the dressing room, I shrugged out of my clothes, unzipped the side of the dress, and stepped into it, wiggling it up into place. I sent up a silent prayer as I zipped it up and turned to see how it looked. Wow. The dress was obviously made with magic. It made me appear to have hips, and it was cut so low that it made my insubstantial cleavage look like actual cleavage. That was never an easy task.

Grinning, I stepped out of the back and twirled around. "Well, what do you guys think?"

They glanced up from the shoes they were looking at, and their mouths dropped open. "Holy shit!" Alexis uttered, clearly in shock.

Second that," Claire said, smirking like the cat that ate the canary. "I told you, Sapphire!"

I sighed. "So you did. Should I try on the black one?"

"No," Alexis said. What you need to do is to go throw away every pair of sweatpants you own. You're only allowed to dress this way from now on. Right, Claire?"

"You'll hear no complaints from me," she answered. "What size shoe do you wear, Sapphire?"

"Eight. Sometimes, seven and a half."

She ran her finger down the sizes on the front of the boxes and pulled out a pair of eights. "Put these on."

I slid my feet in the stilettos and wobbled across the room. "I'm going to break my neck."

"Yeah," Alexis agreed. "But you're going to look fabulous while doing it."

"Great," I groaned. "You'll make sure that makes it on my headstone, won't you?"

***

After the dress shop, Alexis took me to get a blowout— something I'd never done before. My grandmother would roll over in her grave if she knew I spent forty dollars, plus tip, to have someone blow dry my hair. She wasn't frugal, but she wasn't frivolous either. I seriously didn't get how Alexis could do this

39

kind of thing every week. Well, maybe I could understand it a little. I did leave the salon looking like a supermodel.

"Tobias isn't going to know what hit him," Alexis assured me, admiring my long brunette locks. "If he can speak more than gibberish when he sees you, I'd be very surprised."

"I wish I had your confidence."

"When I get done with you, you will."

"Why?" I asked warily. "What are you going to do?"

"Well, first, I'm going to make you shave the woolly mammoth off your legs, then I'm going to do your makeup."

"I'll shave, but I draw the line at makeup."

"Come on, Saph. You'll survive me putting on your makeup and about a billion other things before your puny human life is over."

"Thanks. That's super reassuring, Alex."

She opened the salon door and hustled me outside. "If I don't keep you grounded, who will?"

"Someone with tact?" I suggested.

"There's someone in Everlast with tact?" she deadpanned.

I glared at her. "Oh, you're hilarious. Maybe you should try amateur night at the comedy club."

"Shut your sassy mouth, or I'll tell Tobias that you *lurve* him and want to have his vampire babies."

"First, I'll kill you if you tell him that, and second, most vampires can't have kids. If they could, you'd have a house full of suave half-Irish, half-Stepford children by now."

"Hey!" Alexis exclaimed. "I resemble that remark."

"Which is why I said it, genius."

"Look, are you going to let me do your makeup or not? It'll be dark in a couple hours."

I looked at my watch. "Shit. How did it get to be so late?"

"That's the price you pay for beauty, my friend."

"So," I smirked. "You're telling me that it takes you all day to look like you do?"

"I really need to shut up, don't I?"

"Uh, yeah. I've been trying to get you to do that for ages."

She rolled her eyes. "Do you have foundation?"

"Under the house?" I asked, confused.

"We're going to have to go back into the mall."

"Why? Didn't we listen to enough choruses of We Wish You A Merry Christmas while we were in there before?"

"You asking that perfectly illustrates your need for a trip back into the mall." She grabbed my arm and dragged me toward the double doors. "Let's go. Where's your sense of Christmas adventure?"

"Christmas adventure? Oh, I'm going to hate this, aren't I?"

"Most likely," she said, pointing at the door. "Now get in there."

***

At nightfall, I carefully walked in my stilettos to Tobias' door. I was extremely aware of how much skin I was showing and how much makeup was caked on my face. Alexis had assured me that I looked like a million bucks, but I couldn't trust her to tell me the truth. She would have told me anything to get me out of the house tonight. After all, she'd spent a good portion of the afternoon plucking my eyebrows to perfection.

Holding my breath, I debated running back to the safety of my house, then I stepped up onto his steps and rang the doorbell before I lost my nerve.

A strange man … well, vampire came to the door after only a few seconds. "What do we have here?" the stringy-haired blond vampire asked. Of course, it was in that classic douchey voice that was like nails on a chalkboard to me.

"I-I, uh, is Tobias home?" I stuttered, backing up a step when Mr. Smarmy and Unclean licked his lips.

At the sound of my voice, Tobias jerked the door open wide and said, "I'm here, Saphir."

"Saphir?" Creepy McCreeperson asked. "Aha. So this is the human I've heard so much about. Kinane did not mention her absolutely delectable scent." He breathed in my perfume with a predatory gleam in his eyes, all while positively leering at my measly B cup.

"Calm yourself, Alan!" Tobias warned, then he grabbed him by the collar and jerked him back inside. "Saphir, I thank you for the return of my garden hose, but you needn't have come to the door. I would have noticed its return."

Confused, I stared at him for a long moment until I finally realized what he was doing. Mr. High and Mighty Vampire didn't want anyone to know that he'd asked me out. Well, fuck him. I mean, really. Fuck. Him. Turning on my heel, I walked away without another word.

Infuriated to the point I was talking to myself, I made a beeline to Alexis' house and her extensive wine collection. I knew booze wouldn't make anything better, but it would make me forget for a little while. And I needed to forget. All I could think about was Tobias and the sweet things he'd done to win me over. What happened to that guy, the adorable one that made me a cake?

I sighed. It didn't matter. Tobias could bake me all the plum cake he wanted. Nothing would persuade me to see him again after that embarrassing bullshit. For Pete's sake, I'd shaved my legs for tonight, and I didn't do that for anyone!

CHAPTER FOUR

Alexis swung the door open with a glass of Chardonnay and a frown after my second incessant ringing of the doorbell. "Am I going to have to walk you to his door?" she asked.

"No," I said innocently. "But if you don't give me that glass, I will rip your arm off, walk to Tobias' house, then repeatedly beat him with the bloody stump."

Her mouth made an 'O' shape. "So things went well, eh?"

"Swimmingly."

She sighed, handed me her glass, and stepped to the side. "Come on in. There's plenty more where that came from."

I grumbled, "There better be," and stepped into the warmth of the house. I was going to need it, a lot of it.

Alexis smiled sympathetically. "Oh, there is, but unfortunately, we have company over, so you might want to take the bottle out to the garden. I've got the patio heaters on."

"Company?" I asked, perking up. "Who is it?" The dress might not be completely wasted if there was a cute guy amongst them.

"Kieran Kinane."

Well, I could forget the 'cute guy' hope. While Kieran was as handsome as the next vampire, he was also a human-hating murderer with major attitude towards me. "Yeah, I'll just take this to the swing."

She smirked. "Thought so. Let me tell Ronan the situation, and I'll join you." She handed me the bottle, started to walk away, then took it back. "I don't trust you to save me any."

"Alex!"

"Well, you've got that 'I'm out of chocolate' look."

I snatched the bottle from her hand. "I'm also out of wine."

She backed away slowly with her palms up. "Easy there, psycho."

"Just hurry up," I told her, huffing in annoyance.

"Two minutes," she called behind her.

While Alexis was gone to tell Ronan how predictably pathetic I was, I kicked off the torture devices I'd walked here in and collapsed in the lush, but thankfully, dry grass of the garden to stare up at the moon. Sighing, I asked the bright sphere, "You'd never disappoint me, would you?"

"Now there's something I don't hear often," an elegant voice said.

I couldn't help the involuntary, heavy sigh that escaped me when I heard that voice. I'd know that slight Irish lilt anywhere. Lifting myself to an elbow, I took a long swig from the wine bottle and glared at the unwelcome intruder ruining my solitude. "Hello, Mr. Kinane."

"Hello, Miss Dragulj," he said, smiling serenely. "May I join you?"

"You own all this, don't you? Sit wherever you like."

Inclining his dark head in thanks, he unbuttoned his suit jacket and went down to his knees next to me, careful not to muss his finery. "Must we fight every time we see each other?" he asked. "I don't want to be your enemy, Sapphire."

I lifted a brow. "You have a funny way of showing it."

"Well, I'm not going to tear down your house. Is that not your idea of a truce?"

"Oh, you're not? Super awesome!" I said, with mock enthusiasm. "Now let's go paint our fingernails together!"

ALL I WANT FOR CHRISTMAS ARE MY TWO FRONT FANGS

The corner of his mouth quirked up. "Ah, how I've missed your sarcasm over the past few months, Miss Dragulj."

"And I, yours, Mr. Kinane," I retorted.

With a dark chuckle, he propped himself up on his side, facing me. "Let us not quarrel, Sapphire. Not when you are so beautifully dressed. I'd like the memory of you looking this perfect to be a good one." He pursed his lips, his green eyes twinkling in the Christmas lights strung from tree to tree above us. "And you know, I think I'd like to look back and remember you smiling at me for once. Do you realize that I've never seen you smile?"

"Do you realize that you've never given me a reason to?" I countered.

"Touché."

We stared at each other for a few seconds, then we both settled on our backs at the same time. I laughed, finding our synchronized movements hilarious after slamming a half bottle of wine.

"We're in sync, you and I," Kieran said.

I didn't look at him, I only said, "You had better not be mocking me, Kinane."

He laughed. "I wouldn't dream of it, lass."

"I didn't think vampires dreamt."

"Not in every sense, but I do have some visions I'd like to see come into fruition."

"Spare me," I said, holding my hand up to stop him. "I've already heard this one."

Kieran turned toward me and moved closer. "Sapphire, if you would give me a chance, you would see that I only have your best interest at heart. I know that you don't want to see your family home torn down, nor should you. I shouldn't have tried to force you."

"Are you being serious right now?" I asked. I was skeptical of the complete one-eighty he was doing. It was so unlike him.

"One hundred percent," he assured me. "Honestly, it was your strength and determination that helped me to change my mind on installing the tennis courts. You put up a very unexpected fight. I was inspired."

"Inspired? Really?" I asked. I was still dubious of his frank confession, but downright elated that he seemed to be serious about not tearing down my house.

"Yes, inspired. No one has ever stood up to me the way you have. They're usually afraid I'll rip their head off. But not you. The last time we spoke, you told me to shove Everlast up my ass. That still makes me laugh when I think of it."

I groaned, totally embarrassed. "I'm sorry. I have no filter."

"No, you don't." He laughed. "I think I like that about you, though. And I have to say, that tough girl persona of yours would be kind of sexy if you weren't always trying to insult me." He smiled as my mouth dropped open in surprise. "Speaking of sexy, what's with the sexy red dress? Although you're dead gorgeous in it, it doesn't seem like the kind of thing you usually wear."

I plucked at a hem and frowned. "It isn't. I had a date tonight."

"And you don't anymore?" He looked at his Rolex. "It's barely seven o'clock."

"Let's just say that things didn't work out."

Kieran shook his head in disbelief. "How could that be possible? Did he see you in this dress?"

"Not only did he see me in this dress, but he also bought it for me, along with everything underneath it."

"Well, that settles it."

"What settles it?" I asked, wary of the swift move he made to get to his feet when he said those words.

He held his hand out to me. "We're going out."

I ignored it in favor of reason and self-preservation. "Out?" I asked.

"Yes! To dinner, dancing … wherever you want to go. I want to take you out."

"Are you serious?"

"Perfectly serious. Why do you keep asking me that?" He didn't wait for an answer. "Look, Sapphire, you're dressed to the nines. I'm in a suit. It's fate. Besides, the effort you put into tonight shouldn't be wasted." He held his hand out again. "Come on, a rúnsearc," he urged. "We can't have that header finding out you're over here sulking. You need to kick up your heels a bit."

I didn't understand half of what he was saying, but he was right. I'd be damned if I let Tobias know that he got to me. The pickings in Everlast may be slim, but I was nowhere near desperate. I slipped my hand into his much larger one. "All right, I'll go with you, but if you murder me, I'm going to be really pissed off."

He lifted my hand to his cool lips and brushed his mouth against my knuckles. "Duly noted."

***

Kieran's driver was in front of Alexis and Ronan's house in record time, far before I was ready to go riding off with him by myself.

"You guys have fun!" Alexis called, waving at us from the porch. I may not have been ready, but she sure was. She was all for me going out with Everlast's most eligible bachelor. One, it would save her from being whined at for the rest of the night, and two, it would give her the opportunity to hear some new gossip from me tomorrow. I suspect she never joined Kieran and me outside for that very purpose.

I waved back with my middle finger when Kieran turned toward her voice. "I'll call you tomorrow, you terrible person."

"Looking forward to it!" she answered brightly, before sticking her tongue out and flouncing back into the house.

"You two have a complex relationship," Kieran observed, as he opened the car door. "Most of the time, you get on like a house on fire, but some nights, such as this, you seem almost enemies."

I climbed into the car and slid over to make room for him. "Opposites attract, Kieran, but that doesn't mean we're not still opposites."

"Care to elaborate on that?" he asked, closing the door.

"Nope. I want to know all about you. Start with where you're taking me," I suggested, sliding my hand around the door handle and holding on for dear life.

"To the Regency Room in the Hotel Roanoke."

"That's pretty fancy."

"So is that dress," he pointed out, grinning at my anxious posture.

"Point taken."

"Relax, Sapphire. I'm not going to eat you."

I gave him a knowing look. "You say that now."

"And I'll be saying it later. I don't drink from donors."

"Really?"

"Really," he assured me.

An awkward pause in conversation rose between us. I laughed at the uncomfortable silence. "I don't know what to say to that."

"Oh, away with ye. You without something to say?"

I shrugged and smoothed out a wrinkle in my dress. Kieran was intimidating. Not only was he a vampire, but he was also in a very different class than I was. He and I were just as much opposites as Alexis and I were, only on the financial and social scale, instead of the level of girliness and triviality.

"Roanoke is over an hour away," Kieran reminded me, eyeing the death grip I had on the door handle. "It's going to be a long ride for you if you're balled up into the corner of the seat and holding on to the door like it's a life vest."

Chagrined, I unclenched my grip and smiled. "I'm so sorry. I don't know what's wrong with me."

The skin around his green eyes crinkled with humor as he took me in. "There's nothing wrong with you," he said. "You're out of your element. That's all."

"Out of my element? The town is mostly vampires, Kieran. I'm in that element every night of my life."

"Yes, but I'm the 'head' vampire. Doesn't that score me some extra scary Dracula points or something?"

I tapped my chin, feigning thought. "Now that you mention it…"

"Sapphire, really, you shouldn't fear me," he said, trying to hide his smile. "You are the very last human I would harm."

"Because of the protests?" I asked.

He gave me an appraising look. "Something like that."

"So," I said nervously. "Tell me about yourself, Kieran Kinane. The only thing I know about you is that you're Irish and that you practically charmed the pants off of the reporter who was interviewing you the last time I saw you on TV."

Bemused, he opened the bar and grabbed two glasses. "I can assure you, there was no clothing removed by either one of us when the interview was over. It was completely professional."

"She was totally smitten, and you know it."

He shrugged. "I have no reason to deny it. It happens occasionally. Vampires are well known for their natural appeal. It affects some more than others, as was the case with Maria

Appletree."

"That also explains the vampire pets."

"I detest that phrase, Sapphire. It's demeaning to humans."

"I'm surprised to hear you say that."

He pursed his lips in disappointment. "A fair amount of my reputation is deserved, a rúnsearc, but not all of it. There are many humans that I care about and a precious few that I treasure above all."

I leaned forward in interest. "I'm intrigued."

"As am I."

"About?" I prompted.

"You, of course. You haven't told me anything about yourself. It is your turn to enlighten me."

"There's not much you don't know."

"Untrue," he said. "I barely know anything about you. Tell me your likes and dislikes. Start with your favorite drink."

I perused the many bottles of liquor in the built-in bar and shrugged. "Jameson is fine."

"I have everything. You don't have to drink what I'm drinking."

"I'm not settling, Kieran, I promise. Whiskey is fine."

"You're my kind of woman, Miss Dragulj," Kieran said, grinning as he handed me the drink he'd poured for himself.

Blushing, I watched the moonlit scenery fly by the car window while he finished pouring a second drink.

He relaxed back into the plush leather seat and waited for a few beats before asking, "Have I embarrassed you?"

"Not at all," I told him, though I had trouble meeting his eyes. "Why do you ask?"

ALL I WANT FOR CHRISTMAS ARE MY TWO FRONT FANGS

"Because I have a feeling that I might before the night is over. I have had something on the tip of my tongue since I stepped into Ronan's backyard tonight."

"What is it?" I asked.

His black brows furrowed together as he pondered what he wanted to say. I waited with bated breath for him to continue, trying hard to ignore the sexy stubble on his face. Kieran had always been undeniably handsome, but as he hesitated, looking more nervous than I'd ever seen a vampire look, I wondered if I'd missed something as obvious as his perfection.

"You can tell me," I said, attempting to help him along. "I can take it."

"It's nothing like that, Sapphire. How could I have anything negative to say about you? You are a saint, an innocent."

"Then tell me what it is, Kieran. You're freaking me out."

"It's just that you..." He trailed off as he took my hand and examined how small it was in comparison with his own. "Sapphire, I find that I have never met your equal. Do you realize what a treasure you are?"

I stared at him. "Who are you?"

"A man that knows a beautiful woman when he sees one. When I found you in the garden tonight, I wasn't sure if my eyes were deceiving me. I'd never seen anyone so beautiful in my long life."

Shaking my head in disbelief, I said, "If you knew how long it took to make me look like this, you might reconsider that statement."

He pressed my hand between the two of his, his eyes guileless and earnest. "No, Sapphire, I wouldn't. I think you're gorgeous, even in sweats and a ponytail."

Instead of responding to his apparent lapse of sanity, I threw back the contents of my glass. Coughing from the burn, I held the glass out for a refill. I was definitely going to need it.

"Are you uncomfortable now?" he asked, twisting the cap off the bottle.

"No?" I answered uncertainly. "Maybe?"

His smile was kind but sharp. "That's not what those rosy cheeks are telling me."

"Okay, fine, you caught me. I'm a little embarrassed, but it's only because I think you're kind of beautiful, too. Way too beautiful to be thinking those things about me, I might add."

"Again, that's untrue," he said, topping off the glass. "So you think I'm beautiful? Do tell."

"Well," I said. "Take your arms, for instance. They're so strong and muscled under that suit. What were you in your past life, a farmer?"

His eyebrows rose in surprise. "No, but I did carry my fair share of feed bags and hay bales. I was a stable hand."

"Stable hand, huh? That explains a lot."

"Does it?"

"Yeah, you have a gentle but no-nonsense way about you. I can see you being good with horses with your temperament."

His face lit up. "How easy it is for you to read me, Sapphire. You're right, I did enjoy working with the horses, and the work did build me up. I was a bit of a scrawny lad in my youth."

If that was true, you sure couldn't tell it now. He was tall, stately, a nearly perfect specimen of a man. "I just can't imagine you scrawny."

Kieran raised his brows with interest as I moved closer to where he sat, but he didn't move away. "I was small for my age," he said, shrugging.

I lifted my hand toward his arm as if I was going to pet a rabid dog. "May I, Kieran?"

"May you what?" he asked warily.

"Touch you."

He seemed surprised by the request, but amazingly, he gave me the go ahead with a nod. "Do your worst."

Without taking my eyes from his, I slipped my trembling hand into his suit jacket and slid my palm across his collarbone to his shoulder then brought it down his chest to his stomach. "Kieran, if a vampire's allure is unnaturally strong, how can you ever be sure a woman is really attracted to you?"

"I can't," he said, his voice soft and mesmerizing. "Which is why I am rarely seen with a woman."

"I think the absence of a love interest just makes you more mysterious," I said honestly.

He laughed. It was a deep, genuine laugh that went all the way to his eyes. "You flatter me, Sapphire, and I think I rather like it. Go on. What else do you think about me?"

I rested my hand on the taut muscles of his abdomen. "What else can I say about America's least creepy and most desirable vampire elder?"

Kieran rolled his eyes. "Oh, come now."

"What do you mean, 'oh, come now'? You have to be aware of how powerful and handsome women think you are."

"Are you one of those women?"

I shot an 'are you serious' look at him and said, "One hundred percent, yes," without even thinking about it. The alcohol was making me bold, much more so than usual.

"You honor me, Sapphire."

"And you're being kind," I noted.

He caught my hand as I moved away. "I'm not being kind. I'm being honest, and maybe, a little selfish. I have to admit, I have long wanted to mend our relationship, and if that means I will have your hands on my body, so much the better. You know my feelings on your beauty."

Well, I certainly did now.

***

Three courage bolstering drinks later, we arrived at the hotel.

Are we here already? I said to myself. In between Kieran's tales of his youth on the outskirts of County Laois and my longwinded stories of Peach, I hadn't noticed the time flying by, and truthfully, I wasn't really ready to give up our little bubble of privacy. It was nice, talking to him without the hostility.

I marveled at the beautiful but intimidating structure looming over us as I accepted the driver's hand and stepped out of the car. Without the window's obstruction, it was almost too much to take in. Awestruck, I murmured, "It's magnificent, Kieran."

"It is," he agreed, leading me inside. "Are you ready for dinner, or shall we have another drink at the bar?"

"I should probably eat something," I told him. If I put any more liquor on my empty stomach, it was pretty much guaranteed that I would make a bad judgment call. Touching Kieran in the car had made me ache in places I'd nearly forgot about.

"Very well," Kieran said, pulling me out of my thoughts and reminding me that he was there with a hand on my elbow to direct me.

"Ah! Mr. Kinane! How good it is to see you tonight!" the maître d' exclaimed when he saw us arrive in the dining room. "Should I have the staff ready your room, or will your guest be dining tonight?"

Vampires couldn't blush, but if they could, Kieran would have been bright red after the maître d' finished speaking. "Just dinner,

Thomas, thank you. I'll have a Jameson and water, and she'll have...?"

"Same, but straight up, with a glass of water on the side," I answered.

Thomas seated us and departed in search of our drinks. I took the opportunity to tease my date while we were alone. Smirking at the mortified expression he was still wearing, I asked, "So, Kieran, tell me, do you bring women here often?"

"No!" he said defensively. "I keep a room here in case of an emergency."

"What kind of emergency?" I wriggled my eyebrows.

"The sun, Sapphire."

"Oh."

The second awkward pause of the night was interrupted by Thomas and our drink order. He handed me a menu. "I'll give you a few minutes, miss."

"Wait, Thomas," Kieran called out. "Can I order for you, Sapphire?"

"Go for it," I said, more than a little surprised at the request. "I eat everything."

He handed the menu back to Thomas. "She'll have the filet, mashed potatoes, and creamed spinach."

Grinning at his perfect choice, I asked, "How did you know that I was a meat and potatoes kind of girl?"

"Because you're the perfect wife for an Irishman. Ronan has always said as much, and I could tell myself when you ordered the whiskey."

"I'm obviously living in the wrong country," I said, laughing heartily at his far-fetched assumption.

"I think I like you just where you're at. You're looking a fine thing tonight. I would love to see you dance in that dress."

I glanced at the other couples dining around us. "But no one else is dancing."

"So?"

"So, I'll be embarrassed."

"Sapphire, how am I to make this a date to remember, if you're reluctant to my every offer of chivalry?"

"Is that what this is? A date?"

"Well, yes."

I leaned across the table and slipped my hand into his. "Then I better dance with you, Mr. Kinane."

His smile was radiant. "I would be honored, Miss Dragulj."

Kieran stood and bowed, before kissing my hand and spinning me out of my chair and into his arms. Wow. He was insanely smooth. His polished moves elicited a sigh, not only from me but from every woman in the room. I'm sure that they, like me, thought men like this only existed in movies.

"You are really, really good at this dating thing," I told him.

"I'm a little relieved to hear you say that," he confided, moving me into a sort of rhythmic swaying before skimming his hands down my arms and pulling me closer to his body by my waist. "I'm also glad you came with me tonight."

"I'm glad you convinced me to come," I said, wrapping my arms around his neck.

"I'd love to take the credit, but I believe Alexis convinced you to come, remember?"

"Yeah, but if you weren't so …" I trailed off, searching for an adequate word for the blatant sexual charisma he exuded with every cultivated word. "If you weren't so … you, I wouldn't have come tonight."

ALL I WANT FOR CHRISTMAS ARE MY TWO FRONT FANGS

His eyes widened as he understood my meaning and he moistened his lips. "Your … uh, salad is being served."

I nodded but didn't look away from his full, soft lips. "Okay."

"We should sit," he said, giving me a tantalizing smile that made me weak in the knees.

"Where?" I asked breathlessly.

"At the table?" He didn't sound remotely sure of himself.

"Kieran, I'm suddenly not all that hungry. Can we get them to box the food for me?"

He raised a brow. "Where are we going, Sapphire?"

I smiled shyly. "To your room?"

His eyes darted across the room to Thomas, who sprang to attention like he'd heard his name being called. "Deliver her exact meal to my room in one hour."

"An hour and a half," I corrected.

"As the lady wishes," Kieran said, smirking slightly. "And add a bottle of cognac and Jameson for the room as well."

The maître d' could barely keep the knowing smile from his lips as he said, "Certainly, sir. I shall have them sent up directly."

"Can we take them with us now?" Kieran asked, already walking me toward the bank of elevators.

This time, Thomas' lips did quirk up. "Of course, Mr. Kinane."

***

Kieran waited until we were on the seventh floor and safely in his stateroom to kiss me. It wasn't a passionate, slamming the door closed as we ripped each other's clothes off kind of a kiss; it was a slow, forceful, almost hungry in its intensity kiss. There was meaning in it, a yearning, and it was freaking awesome. I nearly swooned when he gently bit down on my bottom lip with his fangs.

57

It wasn't hard enough to break the skin, but it was hard enough to show me how much he was fighting to control himself with me.

"Are you sure you want this?" he asked, breaking the kiss. "You've had a lot to drink tonight. I don't want you to think that I'm trying to take advantage of the situation."

"Kieran, it's been four years since I've had sex. You will be taking advantage of this situation. Hopefully, repeatedly."

He nipped my lip again. "I'll do my best, you little vixen."

"Yes," I agreed. "You will."

"You surprise me," he told me, chuckling as he walked me back toward the bed. "In a decidedly good way."

"How so?" I asked, trying to suppress a moan of pleasure as his fingertips followed the hem of my dress from my collarbone to my cleavage.

"You're not as I expected you to be," he answered, replacing his fingertips with his lips.

I might have replied, but I honestly couldn't say whether or not I did. When he pushed his fingers into my hair and brought his mouth to mine again, I could barely register a thought. Kieran made me melt in a way I never had before. He was so powerful, so handsome … so ripping my dress apart at the front seam.

"Kieran, there's a zipper on the side," I gasped.

With another sharp tug, my breasts spilled out into his waiting hands, and he grinned at me. "I know."

I reached for his belt, unbuckling it. "You are a very, very naughty man."

"And you are not helping matters," he countered, grinding his teeth together and looking up to the ceiling as I wrapped my fingers around his erection. "Scratch that. Right now, you're brilliant."

I peered down to the impressive length in my hand. "Speaking of brilliant."

He drew his bright green gaze to mine as he peeled off what was left of my dress and hooked his thumbs in my panties. His eyes were those of a predatory animal that had spotted easy prey. "Flattery," he growled, "will get you everywhere with me, Miss Dragulj."

"Will it?" I asked, raising an eyebrow. "Hmmm … let's see then … oh, I know. Mr. Kinane, what if I told you that I love your design for the square and park in front of the post office?"

"Is that true?" he asked, teasingly slipping his fingers into my panties.

"Yes," I said, very aware of how close he was to touching me in a very favorable place. "I sleep under the big oak tree on my lunch break. It's really peaceful there."

"I've seen you do that," he said, easing me down to lay on top of the fluffy white duvet. "And it infuriates me for no reason."

My eyes widened. "So you're a stalker as well as a businessman?"

Propping himself above me, he pressed into me, smiling when it got the reaction he was searching for. "I scan the footage from the security cameras from time to time," he corrected. "The humans of Everlast have an extraordinary advantage over us. Most vampires can't stay awake during the daylight hours."

"Blah blah, blah," I said, rolling my eyes. "Humanity is terrible. Tell me something I don't know."

"Okay." He pushed his palm over my lace-covered warmth, applying pressure to just the right place. "I will buy you every pair of panties in your size at Victoria's Secret if you promise never to put on another pair Tobias has bought for you."

"Deal," I agreed, arching against his hand, then squealing with laughter when he suddenly ripped the crotch out of my ill-gotten panties. "Careful, Kieran!" I cried.

"Oh, now you want me to be careful?" he asked, smiling wickedly as he pushed two slender fingers inside of me. "It's too late for that, a rúnsearc."

A shock ran through my body at the intrusion, and I moaned, dangerously close to orgasm already.

"You're fecking beautiful when you do that, Sapphire."

"Then make me do it again," I said in a breathy voice. "Please."

"Your wish is my command," he growled, withdrawing dexterous fingers in exchange for the insistent pressure of the head of his cock.

As he pushed forward, the pleasant numbness that the alcohol provided evaporated, leaving every nerve exposed and ready to receive whatever ecstasy he was about to bring me. And boy did he bring it. Crying out at the sharp pleasure-pain of his wide girth stretching me to accommodate his size, I dug my fingernails in his back. When he moved into me again, I bit into my lip so hard I brought the coppery taste of blood to my mouth.

Kieran froze mid-thrust, his keen senses picking up on the sight and smell right away. "Sapphire?"

Horrified at the mistake I'd made, I pleaded, "Please, don't stop. I didn't mean to do it."

"I couldn't if I wanted to," he told me, groaning with restraint. "But this does make things harder."

"Harder?" I asked.

"Yes." He withdrew and pushed into me again, this time, achingly slow. "Your blood smells intoxicating. B negative always smells like chocolate to me."

"Chocolate?" I grinned. "Damn, I must smell delicious."

"You do." Leaning down on his elbows, he licked my mouth open and kissed me deeply, before worrying my wounded lip between his teeth. "You taste delicious, too."

"You feel delicious," I said, gripping the taut muscles of his ass to urge him to go faster. At this point, I wasn't the least bit concerned about him biting me. He wasn't as scary as I expected him to be. Maybe it was because he turned out to be a really nice guy, or perhaps it was because he was evoking a much-needed orgasm. It didn't matter which. I'd probably let him bleed me half to death if he wanted, as long as he didn't stop what he was doing right now. Because what he was doing was otherworldly. For a man that could move as fast and flexible as he wanted to, he was exercising great control, pushing into me with a skillful, deliberate speed that set me on fire. My voice was hoarse from the keening cries of bliss that were echoing around the vast room. And then, out of nowhere, I came apart.

There are no words that can describe the feeling of finally having an orgasm that's four years overdue. There are also no words for the two consecutive ones right after it. I'd have to remember to add that to the book, *How to Blow a Human's Mind with Vampire Sex for Dummies*, that I was going to write as soon as I left here. Obviously, Kieran would be my go-to guy for research. He had a real handle on the subject. And might I add, dynamite stamina.

CHAPTER FIVE

The next afternoon, I woke up to Kieran's seemingly lifeless form beside me. He must have trusted me more than I thought he did. Vampires were very particular about who had access to their prone bodies while they were literally dead to the world.

I lifted myself into a sitting position and groaned. I was extremely hung over. The paintings on the wall seemed to be melting, but I was pretty sure Salvador Dali never painted ducks next to the River Thames. I run my fingers under my eyes to see how much of a raccoon I looked like and was pleasantly surprised by how well the waterproof mascara had held up over the eight hours of sex and drinking Kieran and I enjoyed last night.

With a last, lingering look at his nakedness, I made a failed attempt at getting up and ended up on my knees on the floor. "Damn it," I said, laughing at myself as I laid my head on the edge of the mattress. I was fully prepared to sleep down here if need be.

"Where are you crawling off to, Sapphire?"

I looked up to where Kieran was peering at me with one green eye open. "Judging by the way I feel right now, nowhere."

"Good." He turned to face me, pulled back the covers, and patted the bed next to him. "Come here."

It took three attempts, but I made it up onto the bed and curled up with him. I sighed into the dark sprinkling of chest hair and closed my eyes. "With pleasure."

"Pleasure, you say?"

I smiled and reached down to the hardness pushing heavily against my thigh. "You are insatiable, even when you're half dead."

"I blame you," he told me. "You're a sight to behold when you're naked."

Using every ounce of energy I had, I lifted myself up to straddle him and kissed his lips before easing myself down on his erection and throwing my head back in bliss. "You say the nicest things to me, Kieran. Allow me to thank you for them for the rest of the afternoon."

He put his arms behind his head. "Who am I to refuse an offer of gratitude like that?"

"You know, you are a very smart man," I said, grinning down at him.

"Yes, smart enough to know that you have no business being up there." He crooked his finger. "Come here."

I leaned down to kiss him, and he wrapped me into his arms to roll on top of me. "Smooth," I said, laughing at his wriggling eyebrows.

"You were going to make yourself dizzy up there with that hangover."

I pouted. "Yeah, but it was going to be really, really fun."

"And this isn't?" he asked, stopping the delicious movements my body had become so accustomed to in the last sixteen hours.

"Uh-uh-uh." I shook my head. "Don't go putting words in my mouth."

Grinning, he pushed into me with a quick motion that made me cry out. "Would you like me to put something else in there instead?"

"That's how we broke the lamp and got the manager called on us last night," I reminded him.

He scoffed. "That was an honest accident, and it's not my fault that the man next door was seething in jealousy."

"Kieran, he told the manager he thought we were playing freaky bondage games in here. I don't think it was jealousy. I think he was traumatized by how many times I asked you to fuck me harder."

"I think I was traumatized by that," he said teasingly.

I smacked his shoulder. "Asshole."

"He wasn't traumatized, Sapphire. He wanted to see what you look like. That man was listening to us have sex last night and having a very good time while doing so."

"How could you possibly know that?"

"The smell of his lust and envy were overwhelming, even all the way through the wall. Oh, and I could hear him mumbling to himself during the times you were most … vocal."

My eyebrows rose in interest. "What did he say?"

"You don't want to know."

"If you think that, you don't know me that well," I pointed out.

Kieran laughed and sped up his rhythm. "Are you aware my penis is inside of you?"

I slapped my forehead. "Oh, that's why I'm about to come."

"I've never had sex with anyone who talks as much as you do," he told me, ignoring my sarcasm and starting to move in earnest. "I find it distracting but enlightening."

"I've never had sex with anyone who lasted more than four seconds," I retorted. "So forgive me if I'm having a little trouble keeping my thoughts to myself. This whole experience has been enlightening."

"Four seconds? That's very sad."

"I know," I said, my breath catching as I arched into him.

He furrowed his brows as I tightened around him. "Okay, you have about four seconds."

"Way ahead of you," I gasped, before screaming out my completion.

Kieran was kind (or skilled) enough to give me a minute or so to revel in my tenth orgasm in as many hours before his own orgasm followed. Lifting me off the bed with his thrusts, he pounded into me until he growled out his release and collapsed on top of me. "Sapphire," he panted. "Stay with me another night."

I smiled as I ran my fingers through his hair. "If I didn't have to work, I would."

"Quit your job. I'll loan you my phone. Tell them I need you here on my dick."

"Then who would deliver your mail. I'm one of only three people willing to show up, you know."

He sighed. "Fine, but I want you to come straight to my house after your shift."

"Will your cock be there?"

"Yes, he will," he assured me, smiling mischievously.

"Then I'll come."

"Oh, yes, Sapphire, you will definitely do that."

***

Kieran dropped me off in front of my house wearing nothing but his belt and one of his dress shirts at a quarter to nine, and though it was colder than Siberia outside, I couldn't feel a thing. I was happier than I'd been in years. Not only had he spared my grandparent's house from becoming tennis courts, but he had seriously rocked my world last night … and this afternoon. However, the best part, hands down, was that there was none of the drama that was usually associated with an affair. Kieran wasn't looking for anything special with me, and all I wanted out of him was the occasional romp between the sheets. It was a perfect situation for someone with no life to speak of—no pun intended.

Once I was safely inside, Kieran waved from the car and sped away, leaving me to my solitude. I dropped the belt from my waist somewhere in the hallway and was down to the last button of the shirt by the time I made it to the shower upstairs. The blinking light on the phone, the thirty-eight emails I saw on the desktop, all of it could wait until I washed the buildup of styling products from my extremely tangled hair.

"What did you do, Saphir?"

I spun around at the sound of my neighbor's accented voice and jerked the shirt closed. "Tobias! What are you doing here?"

"Waiting on you to return. I was worried about your safety."

"Oh, now you're worried?" I scoffed. "I think you made it pretty clear how concerned you were when you shunned me on your doorstep last night. I spent all day getting ready for our date, you know?"

"And you were breathtaking. That, I can assure you."

"Sure," I harrumphed.

"I promise, Saphir, I had a very good reason for turning you away."

"Yeah, I know. You're ashamed of me."

"No! It's not that. It was the uninvited vampires at my house last night. They aren't what you would call 'human tolerant' unless it's in the capacity of food. I didn't want them to harm you."

"What?" A sharp pain struck me in the heart as my thoughts turned to blind panic. Oh, no. No. No. No! Please, God, tell me I didn't just let another man rip the dress and underwear that Tobias bought off of my body and then proceed to have dirty, animal sex with him all night and half the day for no real reason. I let out a short, horrified breath. "I..."

"It's all right," he soothed, wrapping his arm around my shoulder. "I'm not angry at you. But Kieran? Him, I'm a little pissed at."

Disgusted with myself, I shrugged him off and tore the shirt from my body, not wanting him to comfort me when I was still wearing my 'walk of shame' clothes. I'd done enough to him without making him touch Kieran's shirt. "Tobias, I'm just so, so sorry."

"And naked," he added, amused at the turn of events.

"I'm being serious here, Tobias."

"So am I, completely serious. You are really, really naked."

"You know what I mean."

"I do, but I'm not upset, honestly. I should have told those drecks to fuck off when you came to the door."

"Then why didn't you?"

"I was afraid they would tell you about me, what I've done." He reached out and ran his knuckles down my cheek.

"You mean, the murders?" I asked.

His blue-green eyes met mine. "You know?"

I shrugged. "Since the night you brought me cake."

Realization lit up his face. "That's why you were so nervous around me."

"Well, yeah."

He shook his head. "We've really screwed this whole thing up, haven't we?"

"That's the understatement of the century," I said, agreeing with him.

Walking to the door, he said, "I'll see you after your shower," then left me to recount every sin I'd committed last night.

Left alone with my shame, I turned on the water and started questioning everything I'd done last night. How could I have jumped to a conclusion that sent me to bed with another man so quickly? How could I have been so stupid? And how in the world would I ever make this up to him?

The second I turned the shower off, Tobias handed me a towel around the curtain. "Saphir?"

"Thanks," I said, wrapping myself in the towel he offered and opening the curtain. He was wearing a hangdog expression on his handsome face. "What's wrong?" I asked.

"I lied," he told me.

I tightened the towel around my breasts. "About?"

"It does bother me ... the thing with Kinane."

My heart sank. I knew his quick acceptance wouldn't last. Just like I knew I had probably made the biggest mistake of my short life last night. "It's done, Tobias. I can't change any of it. But if it's any consolation, I regret it. All of it." I looked to the floor. "It feels like I cheated on you."

"That's exactly what it feels like to me, though I realize I don't have any claim to you."

"You do," I corrected, my voice tremulous as I looked into his resolute cerulean eyes. "Uh, did? I don't exactly know where we stand."

"I'm still standing in the same place I was standing when you left yesterday."

Relief flooded into me as I stepped out onto the bath mat. "Tobias,

I'm really sorry that I jumped to the conclusion I did."

He took me into his arms and kissed my wet head. "I should have had the courage to tell you about my past myself. We could have avoided all of this."

I looked up from where I rested my cheek on his white button-up shirt. "Yeah, maybe, but I'm not sure, 'Hi, I'm the new neighbor, and I killed some innocent people,' was the first impression you wanted to make."

"You're right about that." He bit his lip. "Listen, are you hungry? I've got a ton of food going to waste next door."

"You do?"

"I bake when I'm tense. Will you have something?"

"Sure. I'll be right down," I said, unwrapping myself from his person.

"Great. I'll put on a pot of coffee."

"That would be amazing," I told him, and I meant it. After last night's debacle, I needed coffee in these veins of mine—stat.

Tobias left me to dress with a warm, forgiving smile. I sat on the edge of my bed a little stunned. How could I have been so imbecilic? I could have ruined it all. Not to mention, my grandmother would have been horrified by me drunkenly banging my arch nemesis, would-be landlord. Come to think of it, I was horrified by it. If Tobias wanted to break up before we even started dating, I wouldn't blame him.

***

The kitchen table was covered with cakes, cookies, and pastries by the time I felt brave enough to come downstairs. It was incredible. Every square inch was filled with tasty looking desserts that I didn't even come close to deserving.

"Uh, Tobias? Are we expecting company?" I asked him, amazed at the spread.

He held out a cup two-thirds filled with coffee. "I told you, I bake when I'm nervous."

"Yeah, but..." I trailed off, in awe of the complexity of some of the desserts and the vision of Tobias slaving over a hot oven for hours. "I don't think I can eat any of this."

"Why on Earth not?"

I eyed the twin of the plum cake he'd baked me earlier in the week and frowned. "You added the secret ingredient."

He was understandably confused. "What secret ingredient?"

"Guilt."

Laughing, he said, "I promise that these baked goods are completely guilt-free. We both made mistakes last night, and I'm willing to move past them if you are."

I nodded and accepted the cup of coffee. "Are you going to tell me about the … you know?"

"Right now, if you like." He put a serving spoon into the trifle. "What will you have?"

"A little bit of everything? It all looks delicious, and this seems like a good time to eat my feelings."

"Eat your feelings?" he asked, giving me an adoring smile. "You Americans have a lovely way with words."

"Well, you Germans have a way with … uh, you know, I'm just realizing that I know very little about your people, and everything I do know, I'm pretty sure I learned from Nena's *99 Luft Balloons* and beer commercials."

"Then it sounds like you need an education in all things German."

"I guess I do."

He rubbed his hands together and looked excited. "I have several hundred German movies next door if you'd like to see what we Germans are really like. I know most people picture lederhosen and Nazis, but the German people are very much like westerners."

"Bolds words," I teased. "You'd better prove it."

He grinned and grabbed his coat. "I'll be right back."

As soon as he stepped out of the door, I looked at the table and wanted to cry. Tobias was the best man I'd ever known, and I'd stomped all over his heart. I could never deserve him. Sighing, I sat at the table, broke off a piece of pie crust, and shoved it in my mouth. It was good ... really, really good ... probably the best thing I'd ever eaten. I almost wanted to bury my face in it. Nope, I definitely didn't deserve him.

Tobias made it back just in time to see me shoveling a piece of marble cake with a sour cherry topping—another ridiculously delicious selection—into my mouth like I was never going to eat again. "I'm glad you like the *Donauwelle*," he said approvingly. "It was a favorite of mine."

I sighed again and laid my head on the table. "I don't deserve it. You should have made me eat Bratwurst or something."

"So you're saying I'm rewarding bad behavior?"

"Yes!"

"Nonsense," he said, waving away my theatrics.

"Seriously?" I sat up and gestured to the spread. "Black Forest cake? Come on. If that's not a reward, I don't know what is."

He took my hand and led me away from the table, toward the living room. "I think you were right about that secret ingredient thing."

"I told you!" I shouted triumphantly, looking through the stack of movies he'd left on the coffee table. I couldn't make out any of the names. "What did you bring?"

"Romantic comedies. I debated on horror movies just so you'd be inclined to snuggle, but these are better, I think."

"Way better. You know I sometimes faint at the sight of blood, right?"

"Do you? That makes your bringing me a bottle of blood even more remarkable than I originally thought." He stopped walking. "Wait a minute. Do you do that for all of your new vampire neighbors?"

"Yes. Why do you ask?"

"You are very kind, Saphir, too kind."

"Not really," I told him, pulling him down to the couch with me. "It's just ingrained into my DNA to be polite. And I didn't splurge on their bottles of blood like I did yours. They got domestic. Besides, you're one to talk. You're way too kind yourself."

"A match made in heaven then?" he asked.

"Pretty much. Except for that whole immortality thing. Oh, and the blood thing. Gross. You know it's gross, right?"

"I do. So, tell me." He wriggled his eyebrows. "Why did you splurge on my gift?"

"I was hoping you'd be hot. Call me prophetic, but I was right."

Grinning, he said, "You flatter me," and opened the DVD case on the top of the stack. "Where's your DVD player?"

"Upstairs, in the bedroom. I only have a streaming device down here."

"So, you entertain in your bedroom?"

"Nothing but naughty thoughts, I'm afraid. Alexis and I usually watch Netflix down here."

"Do you think any of these will be on Netflix?"

It's possible, but I don't mind watching them up there." I took in his nervous expression with a knowing smile. "Are you afraid to be alone with me in my room?"

He aimed a heated stare at me. "Decidedly not scared. That's why I'm reluctant."

"I promise to keep my hands to myself," I said, drawing an imaginary halo over my head.

He seemed to consider it for a moment, then looked down to the barely concealed cleavage behind my robe. "Better not."

***

We ended up watching *Schlussmacher* and *What a Man*, both starring Matthias Schweighöfer, who seemed to be Germany's answer to Hugh Grant. All in all, the movies were pretty good, and they definitely underscored my ignorance of the German culture. They were so normal, so much like Americans, I had to laugh. "Tobias, I thought you had this sexy, mysterious foreign guy thing going on, but it turns out you're just regular sexy."

"Regular sexy?" he asked. "Where do you come up with these terms?"

"My head. That's usually where the crazy in my life comes from."

He grinned. "Are you telling me I'm now a part of that crazy?"

"I don't think you have a choice, at this point."

"Good," A strange expression crossed his features. Nervousness, maybe? "So, now what?"

"Spontaneous vampire movie night?"

"Seriously?"

"Yep. Scared?"

"A little bit. You're not going to make me watch Twilight are you?"

"Maybe. I make no promises."

We ended up settling on The Vampire Diaries. At first, I sat stick straight on the opposite end of the couch, but after three episodes, I worked up the nerve to stretch out next to Tobias, who was totally relaxed with his big socked feet propped up on the coffee table.

"I was wondering when you'd make it over here," he said, wrapping his arms around me like he'd done it a hundred times before.

"I'm surprised I made it over here at all. Not that I don't want to be here," I added when his face fell. "Oh, hell. I'm going to shut up now."

"You're shy," he said, ignoring my lame attempt at conversation. "I get it. So am I."

I had my doubts about that. Vampires tend to get over their timid tendencies after a couple hundred years on the planet. Although, now that I thought about it, I had no idea how old he was. He could be only a few years older than me. He couldn't have been more than thirty when he died.

"Tobias, is it rude to ask how old you are?" I asked.

"Not at all. I'm ninety years old this coming July. How old are you?"

"Twenty-two."

"Twenty-two?" He sounded shocked. "You are so young."

"Not that young."

"At twenty-two, I wasn't even sure what I wanted to do with my life. Why aren't you out there living it up?"

I laughed. "Because my life isn't a tampon commercial? Oh, and I have bills to pay. I try to get out of town every now and then, but I'm not made of money. I have to think about my retirement."

Impressed, he said, "I wish I had been more proactive in saving. Maybe I'd be better off than I am now."

"You don't have a job, so I'm thinking you must have done something right."

"I do have an extensive investment portfolio, but I am far from rich. I shouldn't have been so frivolous with my wealth when I was younger." He smiled as he mused. "Indeed, frivolous with my life. If I had settled with a wife, I would have had the privilege of seeing my great-grandchildren."

"I take it you're not thrilled with vampirism."

"I never wanted this … this life. To be at the mercy of my sire and the sun for an eternity, it's akin to making a deal with the devil. Albeit, in my case, he is one in disguise."

It was pretty shocking to hear Tobias speak so frankly about his gift being a curse. And that sire business! No one had ever mentioned anything about a sire to me before. Were they supposed to keep that a secret? I thought about the vial of Ronan's blood in my purse. Imminent death or not, I wasn't prepared to answer to a temperamental Irishman for the rest of my unnatural life.

Still thinking about what he'd said, I asked, "If you had to do it over again, would you?"

He sighed and was quiet for a while. "I haven't had much in my life to make losing my humanity worthwhile. Meeting you has been one of only a handful of good memories I could share with you."

"Your sire, he's not very nice, is he?"

"Not in everything he does."

"Are you allowed to tell me who he is?"

"No, but if it weren't an unwritten rule, I would. I can promise that much."

We started watching the show again after that statement, but my mind was elsewhere. Poor Tobias, stuck in a world that he could never escape. On top of that, I had to wonder what that meant for me as his girlfriend. Would I be subject to the same rules as him? There were so many unanswered questions running around in my head. I just hoped he'd be answering them sooner rather than later. Later might be too late.

CHAPTER SIX

There was something on fire. It smelled like burning hair and something acrid I couldn't place. Forcing my heavy eyelids open, I found Tobias fast asleep, his face sizzling in the sunlight coming from my bare windows. For a second, I thought I was dreaming, then realizing what was happening, I bounded up from Tobias' arms and tried to shake him awake, hissing when it singed my hand.

"Tobias!" I screamed. "Wake up!" He didn't budge. I thought back to Kieran saying that some vampires couldn't stay awake during the day at all. Tobias had to be one of them.

Panicking, I kicked the coffee table out of the way and ran to the back of the couch, using all my strength to flip him off to the floor to use it as a temporary shield. I had to get him out of the sun. With my mind whirling, I remembered a can of high heat spray paint under the sink. I'd bought it to refinish my grandfather's barbeque grill before winter set in. I ran full out to the kitchen, grabbed the can, and shook it like a mad woman as I ran to the first window.

A few minutes later, when I was satisfied that Tobias was safe from the sun, I breathed a sigh of relief and ran coughing through the cloud of overspray and smoke to the couch to push it off of him. "Tobias! Wake up! Please!"

He remained motionless.

Screaming under my breath in frustration, I pushed my hair out of my face and started unbuttoning his shirt to gauge the damage. I didn't know what else to do. He had been burned everywhere my body wasn't shielding him, his hands, his face, even his legs. It was bad. Really bad. The more skin I uncovered, the more horrified I became. How could that small bit of indirect exposure cause so much damage?

"Oh, Tobias! Please, please don't be dead!" I cried, getting up from my knees and running to the bathroom for burn ointment and the pair of scissors I kept in the first aid kit. After today's fiasco, I would go to Target and buy enough smoke alarms and first aid kits for every room in the house.

"Okay, I'm back," I said, crouching down to the smoldering corpse on my grandmother's favorite hand-braided rug. "Tobias, it would be super awesome if you would open up your eyes."

With tears streaming down my face, I began to apply the ointment to the worst of the burns. His face and scalp had taken the brunt of the damage. If I weren't crying already, I would have wept over the loss of his golden-tinged brown hair. It was a tragedy. This whole damn thing was. Of all the times I could have chosen to have my drapes dry-cleaned, I had to pick this one. What if Tobias died? Would the vampires blame me? Could I be arrested for this? I shook my head. I couldn't think about that now. I had to have hope.

By the time I'd gently applied the burn cream everywhere but under his boxers, I'd resigned myself to the fact that he probably needed blood to heal. Crawling around to his head, I lifted it onto my knees, pried open his mouth, and with a surge of courage, I dragged the blade of the scissors across my forearm and waited in agony as it dripped into his mouth.

For a few seconds, nothing happened, then he coughed, splattering my face with blood. "Thank God, Tobias! You have to drink. You hear me? Drink, Tobias!"

Without opening his eyes, he grabbed my arm in his iron grip and sank his teeth into me. Instinctually, I tried to pull away, unable to withstand so much pain. It hurt ... a lot... a hell of a lot more than I'd anticipated, but I was amazed to see how fast his burns healed as he drank. After only a minute or two, he was exactly as he was before. It was amazing—a miracle.

However, my relief at his miraculous recovery was short-lived. My arm was still in the strong vise of his hands, and he was showing no signs of stopping his meal.

"Tobias, stop," I said, weakly slapping against his chest with my free arm. "You're taking too much." He strengthened his grip and snarled. "Tobias, stop!" I screamed, panicking as my vision began to blur. "Stop!"

I swung at him as hard as I could then slumped over, my face hitting the cushion of my ruined couch on my way to the sweet state of nothingness. Tobias' bloodied face and hungry eyes were the last things I saw.

***

Losing several pints of blood is strange. I floated in a semi-state of consciousness for what seemed like a few hours. Most of the time, I could hear gibberish, but the rest of the time, I heard Tobias speaking softly to me as he stroked my hair. That was nice.

When I finally became lucid enough to remember what had happened, I opened my eyes to find a shell-shocked Tobias looking down to me. "Don't you ever do that again," he said. "I could have killed you!"

Swallowing dryly, I closed my eyes. "I couldn't lose you."

"What happened?"

"I forgot to pick up my curtains from the dry cleaners yesterday."

"Why am I half-naked and covered in goo?"

Embarrassed, I opened my eyes. "I cut your clothes off to get the burn cream on you. I didn't know what else to do."

"Obviously, you did. Look at your arm."

I lifted the arm and hissed. I couldn't feel it, but my forearm was completely mangled from our struggle and still bleeding.

"Saphir, listen to me. You're going to bleed out if you don't drink my blood."

A wave of nausea passed over me. "I can't. I'll throw up."

"You have to. I promise it will only taste like blood for a second."

"How?"

"Don't question it!" he said, impatiently biting into his wrist and holding it out to me. "You're going to die without it. Drink!"

"Will I turn?" I asked, terrified to be enslaved to someone I knew so little about.

"Not if you hurry."

Though I was more scared than I'd ever been in my life, I did as he asked. For the first couple of seconds, his blood had the disgusting rustiness I'd expected, and I started to gag then the taste morphed into a sweet tasting elixir that tingled on my tongue. It was fantastic, magical. I could actually feel my wounds knitting themselves back together. Hell, I could hear my hair growing. Vampire blood was freaking amazing!

Tobias lifted his arm away the moment I felt completely healed as if he had a second sense for it. "That was weird," I said, sitting up.

He pulled me close, wrapping his arms around me and nuzzling his face into my hair. "Saphir, I was so close to losing myself in your blood. It's so addictive. You could never understand how much."

I pulled away to look at him. "Well, I couldn't just let you die in my living room," I said defensively.

"I am dead," he reminded me.

"Yeah, but…" I started before he put his finger over my lips to silence me.

"Never again. Promise me."

I stared at him a long moment, taking in how perfect he was. "I can't promise you that. It may be the blood talking, but I think I might love you, Tobias."

He smiled, looking both surprised and pleased as he stood to help me to my feet. "That is definitely the blood talking. Come. I'll start the shower for you."

"Thanks," I said, wobbling to my feet. "I'll be there in a second."

Nodding, he turned away but stopped at the stairs leading up to my bedroom. "Saphir?"

"Yes?"

"I think I might love you back."

***

"Are you shitting me?" Alexis screeched, scaring off the pigeons I was sharing my bagel with.

I took a thoughtful bite and chewed. "Nope. That's what he said."

"So, he just came over and told you that he loves you?"

"Not quite."

Alexis closed her eyes in irritation, leaning heavily against the arm of the park bench, then she spoke very slowly as if she was talking to a child. "Tell me exactly what happened from Saturday night all the way until today. Don't leave anything out."

"Okay, okay," I said, giving up. She could get secrets out of MI6 with her knack for badgering. "Kieran and I left your house and went to Roanoke. There, I got completely smashed, and we had passionate, uninhibited sex many, many times. He brought me home on Sunday evening."

"Then what?"

"I found Tobias waiting for me in my house."

"Creepy."

"Not really. He was just upset. Really upset, if I were to judge by the amount of stress-baking he did while I was gone. After I showered, we talked, watched movies and TVD, then fell asleep on the couch."

"And then he told you?"

"Not exactly."

She crossed her arms. "Are you stalling for some reason?"

I sighed. "There was an incident."

"What kind of incident?"

"The kind that could have killed Tobias if I didn't give him my blood."

Eyes wide, she said, "Explain, please."

"I took Me-Maw's drapes in to get them cleaned. I do it every winter before the holidays."

Alexis sucked in a breath. "He burned, didn't he?"

"Yes. I panicked when I couldn't wake him up and gave him my blood. I had to." I shrugged. "Just in case."

"You're very calm about all of this, you know. You can't just tell me you had sex for the first time in four years and that you almost killed someone like you're telling me what you're having for dinner later. Have a little emotion, for heaven's sake!"

"What do you want me to do? Freak out? Believe me, I wasn't the least bit calm when the whole thing went down."

"So," she conceded. "He told you that he loved you after you saved him?"

"No, after he saved me. He almost lost control. I lost a lot of blood."

"Whoa. That's an intense first date."

"Yeah, one for the books."

She was contemplative for a moment, then she asked, "Was King Kinane hung?"

"Shhhhhhh!" I hissed. "He'll hear you! He told me he monitors the town during the day."

"Kieran doesn't care about us," she said, waving away my concern with a manicured hand."

"Yes, he does," I countered, looking up at the camera perched atop the decorative gas lamp next to us. "And we feel much safer knowing that."

"He's not listening, Sapphire. We're lowly humans, remember?"

My phone vibrated in my pocket, and I laughed when I read the text from Kieran.

I'M GLAD YOU FEEL SAFE HERE, SAPPHIRE. THAT MAKES ALL OF THE EFFORT WORTH IT. IF YOU WOULD BE SO KIND, PLEASE TELL ALEXIS THAT I CARE ABOUT ALL THE CITIZENS OF EVERLAST, NOT JUST THE VAMPIRES.

CONGRATS ON THE NEWFOUND LOVE, BTW.

I showed his text to Alexis, who immediately blanched. She looked horrified by what she'd said. "Sorry," she told the camera.

My phone vibrated again. I glanced at the screen.

IT'S NO PROBLEM, ALEXIS.

Alexis stood after I showed her the next text. "I think that's enough embarrassment for today. I'll see you tomorrow to begin our two-week Bitten marathon?"

"Wouldn't miss it. What else would I do on my vacation?"

"Okay, see you later!" she called, already halfway to her car. No doubt, she was late for another hair appointment, or bikini wax, or whatever she did to fill her day.

"See ya," I mumbled, simultaneously brushing crumbs from

my lap and depositing my trash in the receptacle. I had to book it if I was going to make it back to work before my lunch was up.

Jogging across the empty street, I felt another vibration.

IF YOU DON'T MIND, I WOULD LIKE TO SEE YOU TONIGHT. NO STRINGS. I JUST NEED YOUR OPINION ON SOMETHING. BRING MR. FAUST, IF YOU'D LIKE.

I texted back that I'd see him at six-thirty and wondered what on Earth he could need my opinion on for the rest of the day.

***

My phone started ringing the second I turned off the shower. "Shoot!" I yelled to myself, hurrying out of the tub and into a robe. "I'm coming!" I hustled down the hallway to my bedroom and dumped my purse out on the bed. Sliding the phone unlocked, I asked, *"Hello?"*

"Hallo, beautiful."

"Hi," I said, giggling like a smitten schoolgirl. *"You're up early."*

"I can't wait to see you. When can I come over?"

"Now, or is it tacky to be seen in a robe two days in a row?"

"Not tacky at all."

"Good. Do you think you could drive me somewhere at six twenty-five or so?"

"You couldn't stop me. I don't like you walking at night."

"It's only sixteen blocks, Tobias."

"Through a vampire town, Saphir."

"Says the vampire!"

"Humor me?"

"How will you talk me into it?"

ALL I WANT FOR CHRISTMAS ARE MY TWO FRONT FANGS

There was a knock on the front door. *"Answer the door and find out."*

I hurried down the stairs and unlatched the lock. Tobias took one step in the room before giving me a kiss that knocked my socks off. I actually stumbled when he let go of me. "Wow," I said, my voice shaky.

He grinned. "I missed you."

"It's only been twelve hours since you last saw me."

He kissed my palm. "Twelve hours too long."

"You're laying it on a little thick today, aren't you?"

"Not a bit. I mean every word."

"In that case," I stood on my toes and gave him another kiss. "I missed you, too."

"That, I love to hear."

"Then get used to it," I purred. "There's plenty more where that came from."

"Good. I don't want this relationship to be one-sided." He grinned. "I thought about you all day. I even cooked you dinner. I thought you might be hungry."

"Marry me," I said, teasing him.

He gripped my shoulders, his aquamarine eyes fierce with a different kind of hunger. "The moment you are serious about that proposal, I will."

His reply took the next words from my mouth. I think I might have managed a squeak, before backing that eloquence up with, "O-okay."

"Come." He put his arm around me and led me toward the stairs, barely hiding his grin. "You go get dressed. I'll wait for you next door. By the way, where am I taking you?"

"To Kinane's house." When his face registered shock, then

anger, I added, "He invited you to come with me. He knows that we are in a relationship. He just wants my opinion on something."

"I'm sure he won't mind if you are a few minutes late. Surely, he can allow you to eat before you go."

"I'm pretty sure he will mind," I said, smiling at his adorableness. "You know, you're a little devious, Tobias. I like it."

He tucked my hair behind my ear. "Kieran gained an opportunity when I made my mistake. In the same fashion, I will exact my revenge whenever and wherever I can."

***

Kieran Kinane's house was, of course, the biggest, most impressive house in Everlast. The creator of the town and regional leader of the vampires couldn't live in a hovel, after all. I marveled at the ten foot high wrought iron gate around his acreage from the front seat of Tobias' Mercedes. Kieran was taking zero chances with his safety.

"I hope your drive was pleasant," a disembodied voice said over the speaker at the gate. *"Please, drive on through."*

Tobias carefully maneuvered his SUV through the gate and the perfectly manicured lawn to the front of the house, where Kieran was waiting for us. He cut off the engine, nodded to Kieran, and said, "Try to hurry."

"I promise," I told him, and before I could open the car door myself, Kieran was helping me out of it. Who knew vampires could be so polite? "Thanks, Kieran."

"Of course. Thanks for coming."

As soon as I was through his front door, Kieran started speaking. "Sapphire, I think someone is stalking you." Without further explanation, he showed me to a side table that held his iPad. "Watch this video from a camera situated next to your house. I sped it up so you could see it time elapsed."

ALL I WANT FOR CHRISTMAS ARE MY TWO FRONT FANGS

Eyes wide, I stepped forward and watched the screen in horror. There was a tall man, dressed in all black, walking into my yard. He seemed to be listening to what was going on inside, lingering at the windows for most of his visit, but when the lights went out in the living room, he scaled the side of the house, going directly to my bedroom window, like he'd been there before.

"When was this?" I asked, starting to hyperventilate.

"Three nights ago."

"What?" I was shaken. How many times had I looked out at Tobias' porch light that night, totally oblivious of the vampire hanging on to the ledge? "Do you know who it is, Kieran?"

"I don't. He's mapped out the cameras. He avoids them whenever he can. Was Tobias with you this night?"

"No. Kieran, what if it's not him?" My voice was high and reedy. "It could be half the town. There's no shortage of tall vampires in Everlast."

"Don't worry. Maybe it's harmless. Maybe it's Tobias, and he's just so in love with you, he can't help himself."

"Do you really think he could be doing this?"

"No, but listen, you can't discount him as a stalker with something more sinister on his mind until we know for sure who it is and what their intentions are. Promise me that you'll be careful?"

"You don't have to ask."

"Good. I noticed your windows are spray-painted black. I assume that happened during the incident?"

"Yes. I panicked. I didn't know what else to do."

"It was absolutely genius. I don't think I've ever heard of that particular emergency method before, but you can be sure, I have a can or two hidden around the house now."

"Well, then I'm glad to be of service."

"Sapphire, as much as I applaud your ingenuity, I want you to let me replace your windows with something more secure, something unbreakable with UV protection. Those old windows aren't safe. You don't mind, do you?"

"Normally, yes, but after today, not at all. I'll find a way to repay you."

"You don't have to do that. It would be my pleasure."

"Yes, I do have to do that. Or else, it will feel like it's payment for services rendered."

He aimed a sexy smirk at me. "You better hurry back to Tobias. I'm sure he's getting impatient out there."

"What should I tell him we talked about?"

"Tell him I offered you a job. I am offering you a job. I have the perfect one in mind, and I promise to make it worth your while to work the graveyard shift."

"Graveyard shift, huh. Well, Kieran, you certainly make a job with you sound appetizing," I teased, barely keeping myself from laughing. "But who's going to run the post office if I leave?"

He waved a hand. "Who cares? It's the government's problem. Just think about it, okay?

"Okay," I said, giving it genuine thought. I didn't have anything to lose. I had a vacation coming up. I could try working for Kieran for a week. And if I didn't like it, I could go back to my normal, boring life.

He grinned. "Great! I'll put together an employee packet for you to look over.

I smiled tentatively. "Thanks, Kieran."

"It should be me thanking you," he told me. "I have a good feeling about you. I think you'll be a good person to have around." He pursed his lips, looking focused. "And in the interest of keeping you around, until we find the culprit, I want you to promise me you'll be careful about your safety and surroundings. You should always keep a weapon at your side. I want you to say it."

Eyes wide with fear, I recited, "I'll be careful and always have a weapon at my side."

"Very good." He turned to go up the stairs where a woman was just coming down with a clipboard. "Have a nice evening, Sapphire."

"I'll try."

CHAPTER SEVEN

I tried to act as normal as I could on the ride back to my house, but I couldn't stop thinking about the stranger on the video. Sure, it could be Tobias being overzealous in his admiration, but I didn't think so. The man in the video had been ominous and menacing, even his posture had been angry. He scared me. It was apparent I was going to need a dog if I was ever going to be able to sleep again.

"I've been invited to attend a party tonight," Tobias said, bringing me back to the present. "Would you go with me?"

"Depends. Is it casual or dressy?"

"Casual. What you're wearing is perfect."

"Then, yes. I'd love to." I honestly could have kissed him for not taking me back to my house. I didn't think I could face it right now … or ever again. I shifted to get a better look at his profile. "Speaking of perfection, why don't you take a look in the mirror?" Lord knows I was appreciative of what he'd find. Tobias was so damn yummy. The way his bottom lip was slightly smaller than his top, the way a tiny amount of his golden chest hair peeked out of the V-neck t-shirt he was wearing—wow, if we were talking perfection, he had it in spades … and then some.

"I like your eyes on me," he admitted.

I shrugged. "Well, the view is pretty sweet."

He grinned. "You flatter me, Saphir."

"Likewise."

***

I'd listened to vampire pets wax poetic about fancy vampire parties for years. Now that I'd actually attended one, I could safely say they have grossly exaggerated the excitement. I wasn't at the party for ten minutes before I decided that gnawing off the arm that Tobias held was a perfectly acceptable means of escape. The vampire pets must have had their brains sucked out of their heads along with their blood if they thought this was an interesting way to spend an evening.

These people, vampires, whatever you want to call them, were just so boring. All they spoke about was money; how they got it, how they spent it, who didn't have it, and who spent too much of it. They were definitely not my kind of people. My people were probably sitting at home reading a romance novel right now.

"Don't worry. We'll only stay a few more minutes," Tobias said, squeezing my hand in reassurance. "I just want to meet the couple that invited me. They're new in town."

"Good," I whispered. Maybe we could get out of here before someone recognized me as the bane of their existence. "Thank you," I mouthed.

"You're welcome. I think I see your cherubic friend, Alexis, coming this way."

I stood on the tips of my toes and tried to see over the mass of vampires. I couldn't see a thing. Everyone in the room was so tall. Even the women towered over me in the five-inch stilettos they were wearing with their business suits. Well, except for Alexis. She arrived wearing flats with a tasteful pink polka dotted flare dress and fitted cardigan.

Hi," she said, smiling brightly at us. "What are you doing here? You never come to these shindigs."

"That's because I'm never invited," I answered, with a little more sour than sweet in my voice.

"That'll be the reason," she agreed, plowing through to her next question, which was the same question she'd just asked. "So, what are you doing here tonight?"

"Counting the seconds until I can run screaming from this

room?"

"She was invited," Tobias said, interrupting what was sure to be a sarcastic reply from Alexis. "The invitation said I could bring a plus one, and here she is. I'm Tobias Faust, by the way. You must be…" He gave me a questioning look. "Let's see …beautiful blonde hair, big blue eyes … this must be Alexis Seward."

"Guilty!" she said, preening under his effortless charm. "Sapphire has told me all about you."

"Has she?" He smiled my way, before frowning at the group behind us.

"That's the blood bag across the street that won't move," I heard the woman standing closest to me whisper.

"Who's the handsome stranger?" her friend whispered back.

"Tobias Faust."

"Is he rich?"

"Isn't everyone in this town?"

The friend glared in my direction, showing fang. *"Almost everyone."*

"I think it's starting to feel a little clownfish in a sea of sharks in here," I whispered.

Alexis laughed. "Is that a Finding Nemo reference?"

"Whatever gets me out of this house," I told her.

"Not everyone hates you here, Sapphire. Ronan and Tobias, for starters. Oh, and Obsidian and Korrina, of course."

"Out of my way!" A southern accented voice shouted. "What don't y'all understand about 'Excuse me'?"

I grinned. I knew that voice anywhere. It was my friend, Korrina. She came out of the crowd looking harassed but gorgeous in a formfitting black top and a full gauzy red skirt. No shoes, though. Nymphs detested them. They preferred to be close to nature when they could.

"Sapphire, girl, they hate you here!"

"Tell me about it." I rolled my eyes. "It's because I won't sell the land to let them build tennis courts."

"No, it's because they're douches," she corrected, giving a shocked guest an irritated look. "You heard what I said. Douches."

Barely keeping the smile off my face, I asked, "Should we go outside to talk?"

"Why? This is my house. They can leave."

The vampire that received the brunt of her tirade did just that, and several others followed her.

I grabbed her arm. "Does that mean what I think it means?"

"Yes!" Korrina did an impromptu happy dance. "We got the business loan!"

"I'm so happy for you!"

Korrina and her husband Obsidian were truffle hunters. They traveled all over the world to find the little fungus delicacies. Truffles were big money. Chefs would pay tens of thousands of dollars for the right ones. Right now, they were concentrating on the burgeoning popularity of the pecan truffles found in pecan groves. The old grove on the back of my land was full of them, which is how we knew each other. She knocked on my door on a cold winter night, not unlike tonight, two years ago and offered me five thousand dollars to let her dig them up. I accepted, and we'd been friends ever since.

"Oh, where is Obsidian!" she exclaimed. "He was hoping to see you tonight."

"I haven't seen him, though it might be easier to find him now that everyone is leaving." Her outburst had had the desired effect. The crowd was definitely thinning out.

She shrugged at the mass exodus with a twinkle of mirth in her grass green eyes. "Oh, well. They were only here to gawk at the 'true vampire', anyway. So," She glanced at the vampire who's hand I had in a death grip. "Who's the lucky fellow, Saph?"

"Oh, shoot. Where are my manners? This is my neighbor, Tobias Faust. Tobias, this is my friend from Alabama, Korrina Raines."

"Hello, Korrina. It's a pleasure to meet you." Tobias shook her hand but didn't linger over it like most men do. Korrina was very, very beautiful. Something that was not at all uncommon for nymphs ... or really, for vampires, and she was both. "Saphir," he whispered. "Are you okay to stay now?"

"Sure, unless you want to leave."

"I am content to stay as long as you like." He gestured around, smirking at the absence of superior attitudes. "The atmosphere seems to have lightened up considerably."

I laughed. "That it has." The room was a ghost town at this point. "Korrina, why did all of those jerks get an invitation when I didn't. I might be a little hurt by this."

"Alexis," she told me, jerking her thumb in her general direction.

"Korrina!" hissed Alexis. "Don't you dare!"

Korrina pushed the mass of long dark curls from her face. "Hey! I'm not going to lie for you. This is your experiment, crazy woman."

I put my hands on my hips and glared at Alexis, eyes narrowed to slits. "What did you do?"

"Nothing," she promised. "Honest!"

"You're worse at lying than Korrina is at keeping a secret," I told her.

"Hey!" Korrina yelled.

ALL I WANT FOR CHRISTMAS ARE MY TWO FRONT FANGS

"What's all the ruckus?" asked a tall, dark-haired, and ridiculously handsome vampire as he put his arms around Korrina and gave her a peck on the cheek.

"Obsidian, your wife is involved in another of Alexis' parodies of a secret mission."

"Secret mission? That's absurd." He shook his head and held a hand out to Tobias. "Hey, man, I'm Obsidian Raines. Has Korrina told you what a fantastic girl our Sapphire is?"

"You, too, Obsidian?" I hung my head in mortification. "Am I really that pathetic?"

Tobias answered for them. "No, you're perfect, remember?"

I smirked. "Oh, yeah. That's right."

"You don't have to sell me on Saphir," Tobias said, addressing the group. "I'm going to make her my bride as soon as she accepts my hand."

"What the hell, Sapphire!" Alex said grumpily. "I went to a lot of trouble to arrange this, and you're already engaged?"

"I haven't said 'yes'."

She gestured to his hotness. "Are you out of your mind?"

"Can I at least know him for five days before you plan our happily ever after?" I snapped.

"Fine." She crossed her arms. "No."

I threw my hands up. "You're hopeless."

There was a long pause, then Korrina clapped her hands. "We need booze."

"Yeah," I agreed. "A lot of it. And I think I deserve the biggest drink because my friends are all freaking weirdos."

"Alexis only has your best interest at heart," Tobias assured me, as we made our way to the open bar. "I think it's nice that you have friends that care about your future."

"I'm sure you have them."

He frowned. "I am sure that I don't."

"Well, you have me, and while I don't want to set you up with someone, I will do other things for you."

His brows raised. "What kind of things?"

I stood on my toes to kiss him, and everyone in the room wooed and whistled. I took the opportunity to flip them off behind Tobias' back and said, "Whatever you want, Mr. Faust."

"Why does it sound so provocative when you say my name, Saphir?"

"I don't know, Mr. Faust. Why does it?"

"Okay," he said, wheeling me around and walking me towards the front door. "Time to say goodbye."

"Goodbye!" I said to my smirking friends, grabbing a bottle of scotch from the bar as we hurried by.

"Use protection!" Korrina called, before the door shut behind us.

"Protection?" I asked. "I thought vampires didn't have human diseases."

"We don't. I think she meant protection from pregnancy. I am a relatively young vampire."

"Oh," I said, then clamped my mouth shut. I didn't have anything to say to that.

"I have them ... uh, condoms, already ... not that I thought we might."

"You totally thought we might," I teased, nipping at his full bottom lip. "Let's go 'might', Tobias."

"Get in the car," he said, his hunger making his eyes glow amber in the streetlight.

ALL I WANT FOR CHRISTMAS ARE MY TWO FRONT FANGS

Laughing giddily, I jogged to the passenger side and got in. "Hurry up."

Tobias seemed to wake from some kind of stupor and quickly jumped into the driver's seat. "Hold on."

I snapped my seatbelt into place the second he fishtailed out of the driveway and slammed the car into drive. We made it back to his house in twenty seconds.

Unbuckling my seatbelt, he pulled me across the bench seat of his SUV and growled, "Tell me now, if you don't want this."

"Tobias," I looked him in the eye so he'd know I was serious. "I really want this."

Nodding, he placed my arms around his neck and lifted me up so I could wrap my legs around his waist. Smiling slightly at the gasp I made when I brushed his erection, he carried me into the house, straight to the bedroom, and deposited me onto the bed.

With the door closed behind us, my inhibitions seemed to come rushing back to the surface. Could I really do this? Should I do this? I looked at Tobias, really looked at him. He was kind, way more kind than he should be, especially after the Kieran incident. And he was sweet, and gorgeous, and built, and pretty much a golden Adonis, and if all of that wasn't enough, he baked. Yes, I could definitely do this.

Working up my nerve, I patted his dark blue comforter, beckoning him closer. He sat, letting me set the pace. "Tobias, I've never done this with someone I've really liked before. I'm nervous."

"That you'll disappoint me, or that I'll disappoint you?"

"You could never disappoint me."

"I love you," he whispered, before cupping the back of my head and bringing my mouth to his.

I went willingly, the passion my shyness had killed crashing over me like a wave the second his lips touched mine. Hurriedly, I lifted his shirt over his head, and he returned the favor by ridding me of my shirt and bra. When were both naked from the waist up, we stood and kicked off our shoes and pants in a frenzy until we were naked in front of each other for the first time.

"You're beautiful," he said.

I wanted to say something equally as flattering, but I couldn't seem to make sounds come out of my mouth. I ended up lifting my eyebrows and gesturing to his perfect erection in a 'holy shit' way.

He laughed. "I take it you are not disappointed?"

"Will you marry me?" I asked, in answer.

"Is this all it took to get my ring on your hand?" he teased. "I could have made you my betrothed on the night I brought you cake if you'd only told me."

"What can I say? I'm easy to please."

"That has yet to be determined," he said, backing me to the bed with his body.

"And yet, I remain cautiously optimistic."

"Sapphire?"

"Yes?"

"Be quiet."

I had no problem with that. As he dragged his lips up my neck to my mouth, I couldn't have spoken, anyway. Holding my breath, I ran my palms down his furry chest and stomach and took him in both hands, smiling when he caught an unnecessary breath.

"A condom!" he blurted out. "We need one." He looked torn as if he wanted to go get one, but he really wanted my hands to stay right where they were.

Laughing, I let him go and climbed onto the bed. "Hurry."

With vampiric speed, he ran to the adjoining bathroom. I

could hear him searching through drawers first, then cabinets, before he yelled, "FUCK!" to no one.

"What's going on in there?" I called.

He came out empty handed. "How good are you at Monopoly?"

"You're kidding? You can't find them?"

He looked skyward and shook his head. "I am a hundred percent not kidding right now."

"Okay." I slid off the bed and put my shirt on. "But I get to be the car!"

By the time daylight spilled over the mountain, Tobias could barely keep his eyes open. I didn't mind. As I lay there, way past drunk and wrapped up warm in his arms, I was content to stare at the two of him until the sun came up. It was absurd how much I liked him after such a short time.

His eyes popped open. "If I fall asleep, are you going to put makeup on me?"

"No, but I might put your underwear in the freezer."

He smiled sleepily. "I'm not wearing any."

"Are you trying to kill me?"

"I don't think me being naked is going to cause you harm."

"We'll see."

He yawned. "Will you be here when I wake up?"

"If you want me to be, I will. And unlike you, I'll have condoms."

"Thank God." He yawned again. "I love you."

"If you loved me, you would have had condoms in the house last night," I griped.

"That particular predicament will never be duplicated. As soon as I rise, I'm going to Sam's Club to buy a case of them."

"A case?"

"A case," he assured me, smirking at my raised eyebrows. "Are you afraid?"

"No. Obviously, you're planning a huge water balloon fight. I'll have you know, I've got great aim."

Laughing, he shook his head. "I believe it."

***

A knock on Tobias' door woke me soon after we went to sleep. Sitting up, then immediately regretting it, I glanced at the clock that seemed to be hovering over the nightstand as the room spun around it. How much did we drink last night?

"Wake up!" I hissed, shaking Tobias' shoulder, though I knew it was fruitless. He'd had more to drink than I did, and there was that whole 'can't stay awake in the daylight' thing.

Sighing at Tobias' peaceful face, I got out of bed and nearly fell headlong into the dresser when I tripped over his pants. Damn, I was glad he wasn't awake to see me naked and on my hands and knees as I looked for my clothes. I suffered enough embarrassment last night when I gave him an impromptu lap dance to *Lady Marmalade*.

Giving up the clothes hunt, I pulled on Tobias' shirt and ran to the peephole to see what all the commotion was about. In the driveway, there was a Lynchburg County Sheriff patrol car, and on the porch, a graying deputy who was looking extremely nervous. He demeanor said that he knew that this was a vampire's house and that he was none too thrilled to be here.

Cracking open the door, I crossed my arms in front of my breasts and asked, "Can I help you?"

"Are you Sapphire Dragulj?" the deputy asked.

ALL I WANT FOR CHRISTMAS ARE MY TWO FRONT FANGS

"Yes." I pulled Tobias' t-shirt down in the front. "What's going on?"

The deputy looked at the general state of me, then he smiled. "I'm guessing you haven't been home today."

"No, I …" I trailed off as he pointed out the side of my house from where he stood. "What the fuck?" I cried, pushing past him to walk to my yard in disbelief. Someone had spray-painted *SLAG* in big, black letters between the living room and kitchen windows. I was sure that was British slang for whore. Just great. Someone out there thinks I'm a whore, and even better, they weren't shy about sharing it.

"There was a vandalism call from one of your neighbors just before daybreak," my personal harbinger of doom continued. "Do you know they actually demanded that it be removed before they wake tonight. The nerve of these bloodsuckers!"

I started to laugh. Not at his slur, but the absurdity of the situation. It was too ridiculous. I was a good person. I was polite, friendly, and went out of my way to make the vampires comfortable with me, and this is what I got from them? "Well, that's awesome … exactly what I wanted to do with the mother of all hangovers."

"Alrighty, I'll try to move this along then. Do you have any idea who could have done this? Any jilted ex-lovers or boyfriends? Maybe one of their wives?"

"This graffiti isn't accurate," I said, glaring at him, but even as I said the words, I knew they weren't true. As much as I'd like to tell myself that I wasn't acting like a slut, I sure as hell wasn't acting like a lady. I'd spent the night with Kieran only two nights ago, then almost immediately after, I went to the party with Tobias. Any of my neighbors, or Alexis and Ronan's neighbors, for that matter, could have seen me and felt strongly enough to do this. My grandmother would be disappointed with the shameful way I was acting.

"All right, we won't take up any more of your time," the deputy said. "If we find the culprit, we'll be in touch."

"You don't expect to, do you?"

"We don't have the resources to track down every spurned lover who acts out, Miss Dragulj, and if this turns out to be a vampire, there's not much we can do. It's out of our jurisdiction."

"That's reassuring," I said sarcastically.

"That's the world we live in now, miss. Maybe you could try asking Kieran Kinane. He might be able to help you better than we can."

I sighed inwardly. "Yeah, I'll call him tonight."

The deputy pursed his lips. "I'll tell you what. If you find out who it is, or if something else happens, give us a call. We'll try to help. Oh, and you can pick up a copy of the police report at the station a little later for your insurance claim."

"That won't be necessary. I'm going to take care of this myself."

I turned to march straight for the shed to get the pressure washer. I knew it was a longshot, but I didn't have a backup plan that didn't involve going to Home Depot for paint. I was both praying and crossing my fingers that my garden spigot's pitiful water pressure would be enough to erase my new favorite spray-painted expletive and that the discount pressure washer I'd bought could handle something like this. So far, the worst thing it had faced was the year I didn't pass out Halloween candy. Judging by the amount of egg it helped me wash off the side of the house, grieving for a loved one wasn't an adequate excuse for the kids of Peach. Snickers and peanut butter cups were infinitely more important to them than the woman who raised me.

"Uh, Miss Dragulj?" the deputy called.

I turned around, impatient to get the atrocity off my grandmother's house. "Yes, sir?"

He smiled again, his kind eyes crinkling with crow's feet at the corners. "First, you might want to think about pants."

I looked down to my bare legs and sighed, suddenly realizing how freezing cold it was. "Yep, you're right. Pants are first."

Thanks to a heavy icy fog that inhibited the paint from curing, I was able to shower after my super fun-filled, but successful morning activities with peace of mind. I may not know who my stalker is, but I wouldn't have to deal with irate vampires come nightfall, and that was fine by me.

When I was done, I dressed in my most business-y of business suits. It was high time I paid King Kinane a visit. Not only was I dying to see the footage of the foulmouthed vandalism suspect, but I wanted to find out what job he could possibly want to give me. Whatever it was, it was a blessing. It would be vampire hours, which meant I would be able to spend a lot more time with Tobias. Plus, I would probably get a raise. That meant I could afford those all-important bear traps I so desperately needed around my house.

***

About an hour before sundown, I sent a text to Kieran.

ARE YOU AWAKE?

His reply was immediate.

YES.

CAN I COME OVER? THERE ARE SOME THINGS I'D LIKE TO TALK ABOUT IF YOU HAVE THE TIME.

I'M AT YOUR DISPOSAL, SAPPHIRE.

GOOD. I'M AT YOUR GATE.

I KNOW. COME IN.

Laughing, I twisted the knob on the gate when it buzzed and walked straight into his house. Somehow, I didn't think he'd meet me at the door. "I'm here," I called, shrugging off my coat and hanging it on the rack.

"Thanks for remembering that I can't answer the door."

I motioned around me. "Vampire town, remember?"

"I seem to recall something along those lines," he joked, with a handsome grin on his face. "What brings you here today?"

"I have an agenda."

"An agenda, is it?" He sat on the settee and gave the cushion next to him a pat. "By all means, enlighten me to your plans."

Ignoring his invitation, I started pacing. "Okay, first, someone spray-painted the word, slag, on the side of my house sometime between the time I left here and ten o'clock this morning."

"What?" he asked, alarmed at my news. Obviously, he wasn't expecting anything like that to come out of my mouth.

"Yeah, it wasn't the most pleasant thing to wake up to."

"I imagine it wasn't. Sapphire, I feel like I'm failing you. The community is supposed to be a haven for vampires. There's no reason it can't be like that with the few humans we have here. A vampire's life is nothing but temptation. They should be used to living with humans after three years of being out in the open."

"Kieran, I'm not really a resident. I was grandfathered into the district. And even if I wanted to, I couldn't afford the HOA dues you charge. Six hundred dollars a month, are you insane?"

"You could afford it if you take the job I offered you."

"Funny you should mention that," I said, finally taking the seat he offered. "That's part two of my agenda."

"I was hoping you'd give it some honest consideration." He reached over the back of the sofa and picked up a file folder from the table behind us. "It is a genuinely interesting employment opportunity, especially for someone in your position."

"Really?" I asked, squinting at him in disbelief.

"Why are you always surprised by my more honorable gestures?"

"Because you've tried to convince me to move from my childhood home for two years."

"We will have to move past that if we're to work together every day," he said, smiling broadly at my frankness.

"We're working together? What would I be doing?"

"It's all in the package. Feel free to peruse it at your leisure. I'm housebound for the next hour or so."

"Will I be bored, or doing anything illegal or immoral?"

He chuckled. "Sapphire, don't be silly."

"Well, I doubt it will be in the package. I just want to know now."

"Does that mean you're considering the offer?"

"I could think of worse things. Not many, but a few."

"You wound me," he said, clutching his chest.

"I'm just kidding. If the pay is right, I'm all yours. In the employee sense, anyway."

"I'm glad to hear it. I need someone like you that can see a human perspective on things in Everlast."

"If all you need is a human view, you could have hired anyone. Why me? It's not because of ... you know, is it?"

"No, lass. It's not because of you know," he said, laughing at my innocence. "I've tried other humans before with disastrous results. No one quite gets it like you do. You know how to deal with us at our worst."

"Tell me about it ... two longest years of my life," I muttered, giving him the most martyred expression I had in my arsenal. "But still, Kieran, I can't be the most qualified person to do this ..." I trailed off, looking at the job title in bold print on the folder. "Director of Vampire-Human Relations? Really? I know I'm not qualified for that."

"You are."

"How so?"

"You aren't afraid of me. I have hired dozens of humans for this position. They, like your colleagues at the post office, are so afraid of all the things that could happen, they won't give it more than a few days before they quit."

"What makes you think I'm not afraid of you?"

"You don't have any qualms about telling me how it is, or rather, how it will be. I can't tell you what a relief that is after so many years of being catered to. You keep my ego in check." He shook his head at my skeptical face. "Do you remember the night we met?"

Did I remember the night we met ... was he kidding? You don't forget the night a centuries-old vampire comes to your door and tells you that it's in your best interest to move. I should have been terrified for my life; Kieran's reputation had most definitely preceded his arrival in Peach, but I wasn't. I was pissed. My grandmother had passed only days before, and he had the gall to tell me I needed to move? In a pig's eye!

Kieran's eyes crinkled in the corners as he watched me. He knew exactly what I was remembering. "I deserved everything you said and more, Sapphire."

"It's one of my favorite rants of all time."

"That's exactly why I need you in this position. The job really just consists of you making sure everything I do is human-friendly and finding amicable solutions for problems that come up in town. You can work in one of the offices here or work from home in your pajamas. As long as you report to me once a night, either is fine."

"Really?"

"Again with the doubt?"

"Sorry, this is all feeling a little surreal."

"Take the job," he suggested, waving away my doubts. "I'll feel better. You'll feel better. The humans in this town will live better. It's a win-win for us both."

I peeked into the folder for a look at the pay and my stomach dropped. It was more than three times my current salary. "I'll take it," I blurted out, without hesitation.

"Great!" he rejoiced, hugging me to his massive side. "You won't regret it. I'm a very easy-going boss."

"We'll see."

He laughed and stood up to make his way back the way he came. "Be here tomorrow evening at seven, and I'll give you your first assignment."

"What about my house art?"

"I'm on it. I'll call you with any news."

"Okay." I stood to retrieve my coat. "See you tomorrow?"

"Tomorrow, a rúnsearc."

CHAPTER EIGHT

Tobias was still asleep when I returned to his house. Exhausted, I climbed into bed next to him, snuggled up to his room temperature body, and rested my head on his chest. He may not be warm, but that wasn't as important as him just being there when I needed someone. Of course, it wasn't as if he could go anywhere.

I sighed. It felt really right in his arms. Even more so since I knew Tobias couldn't be behind the things going on at my house.

"What is it, love?" Tobias asked, his voice thick with sleep.

Nothing but drama, I can assure you," I said, propping myself up on his arm. "Sorry, I didn't mean to wake you."

He pulled me on top of him. "Nothing brings me as much joy as you being in my arms when I wake."

"Wow. I thought you'd need more than thirty seconds to build up to your usual charm level, but this is impressive. Care to elaborate on how you manage that?"

"No. Care to elaborate on your drama?"

"Well, unlike you, I'm an open book. I, Mr. Faust, have a foul-mouthed stalker, who has a penchant for spray-painting insults on houses."

"What?" he asked, sitting up with me in his arms. "What kind of insults?"

"Slag—not too original, but surprisingly effective, nonetheless. I spent the morning pressure washing it off of the house."

"I shouldn't have taken you to the party last night," he said, blaming himself. "This is my fault."

"No, it's not. This started before last night. I've already seen a video of someone peeking into my windows. Not going to the party wouldn't have made any difference."

"You knew about this, and you didn't tell me about it? Are you mad?"

"Kieran only showed me yesterday. That's why he wanted to see me. And besides, I couldn't very well tell you before I ruled you out."

"Wait a minute. You thought your stalker could be me, and you still spent the night here?"

"We are all fools in love," I said, nipping at his lips. "Are we not?"

"That we are, Saphir." He laid back down and pulled me close. "I like you in my bed."

Good, because I'll be in it a lot more often now that I've got a night job. Kieran made me Director of Vampire-Human Relations today. I start tomorrow night."

Aghast didn't really seem to cover the expression on Tobias' face upon hearing my news. "You took a job with Kieran Kinane?"

"Yeah, it was a good offer … triple my pay."

"You cannot trust him," he said, looking more than concerned. "Do not ever think you can."

I rolled my eyes. Kieran was no threat to me. "He's not that bad, Tobias. And anyway, isn't he a friend of yours?"

"He is my maker, and he will be yours if you do not take care."

Alarmed, I climbed off of Tobias. "You didn't think that was important enough to share before now?"

He sighed, looking worried. "Saphir, I need to tell you something."

I nodded, silent. I knew he was about to drop a bomb by the somber look of his sea-colored eyes.

"First, my love, I want you to promise me that you'll give me a chance to explain everything before you react."

"I promise," I said. "Go ahead."

He cleared his throat. "You must understand that the sire bond Kieran and I have is unbreakable. I can never escape him, never tell him no. As long as he lives, I have to obey him."

"Okay. So far, not so bad. Kieran isn't evil, right?"

"No, he is not. Unlike most vampires, Kieran actually lets his children live wherever they desire and only calls on them when he has need of them."

A cold sweat broke out across my skin. "Uh huh … but?"

"He asked me to move to Everlast two years ago, just after he learned that you would be allowed to stay here."

"No." I bolted up from his lap, suddenly wishing I'd never seen the inside of Tobias' bedroom. No matter how this ended, it could not be good.

"It wasn't an immediate thing. He gave me two full years to get my affairs in order, and I was grateful for it. I had a life in Canada … a house, a job, even a cat. I didn't want to come here. After the murders in Germany, I wanted to get away from everything and everyone associated with my past, my maker included. I had that there."

"Where do I come in?"

"Kieran asked me to seduce you into moving out of Everlast."

I was floored. It was as if someone had tilted my little world off its axis. "S-so, that means … everything is a lie, that what we have is a lie?"

Adamant, he said, "No, absolutely not," and stood to calm me. "I do love you. Yes, at first, I would have done anything to sway you, but within a minute of meeting you, I didn't have to fake anything. You were … are beautiful, smart, funny—you're everything to me, Saphir."

"Were you ever going to tell me?"

"No. I was afraid that he would kill you if I failed. I should have realized how silly that fear was. Kieran is in love with you. He calls you his *a rúnsearc*. That means you're his secret love. He would never hurt you."

"I don't know what to say to that." Me? Kieran's secret love? Maybe in some kind of an alternate reality. In this one, no way.

"Don't say anything," he told me. "Kieran approves of our relationship, and with him changing his mind on your land, there's no reason to tell him that you know his secret."

Who was this person? Did he really think I would be okay with him charming my pants off to lure me out of Everlast? "Are you crazy?"

Tobias moved closer. "I know it's not ideal, but I believe we can move past this."

I backed away a step for every one he took toward me. "Say Kieran didn't let me keep my house, Tobias, how far would you have taken this?"

He sat, a wounded look on his face. "I would have married you. There wasn't a choice. For sixty-seven years I have been at Kieran's mercy."

"I need to have a little conversation with Kieran," I said, fuming with anger. I started looking around for my things. "I need to know why he thought this elaborate scheme was necessary."

"He doesn't anymore."

"What do you mean?"

"The last time I spoke with him, he told me to abandon my mission."

"Why?"

He sighed. "I think he's hopeful. After you went to Roanoke with him, he came back a different man."

"A different man," I repeated disbelievingly. "Why didn't he tell me any of this himself."

"You hate him."

I straightened from picking up my jeans and walked out of the bedroom door with my clothes from the night before tucked under my arm. "Yeah," I said, with a voice full of snarky intent. "Because I fuck everyone I hate."

He followed me to the front door, then stepped back when he remembered that it was still daylight outside. "Saphir, please, don't go."

"I'll talk to you soon," I told him, edging my way out of the house and into the bright sunshine on his porch. "I promise."

He spoke from behind the closed door. "I'll hold you to that."

***

As soon as I made it into my house, I collapsed into a puddle of despair. I felt so … well, I couldn't place what I was feeling, but I knew that pissed was at the top of the list of possibilities. How could they have done this to me? Tobias, I could, maybe, forgive for his part, but Kieran, he should count his blessings that I wasn't over there tearing him a new one right now.

"You know what? Fuck this!" I shouted at no one. Kieran did deserve a piece of my mind, and I was going to give it to him.

With a growl, I lifted myself to surprisingly steady feet and marched out the door. I stormed past Tobias' eerily quiet house without a second glance and didn't see another thing until I stood in front of Kieran's gate.

"Back so soon?" he asked when I pressed the intercom under the camera.

"I just couldn't stay away," I muttered, gritting my teeth as I turned toward the sound of the buzzer, pushed through the heavy wrought iron gate, and stomped my way up to his door. Without knocking, I turned the knob and kicked the door open, letting it ricochet off the wall. "Where are you, Kieran?"

"Easy on the hinges," the object of my hatred said, as he made his way down the stairs to me. His face was the picture of confusion as he watched me slam the door shut. "What's going on?"

Almost without thinking, I reached out and slapped him. "How dare you?" I screamed, walking forward as he backed away with a new expression—realization.

"Tobias told you," he deduced.

"Everything!" I spat. "How could you? I mean, how? Why? Do you think you're God? You can't play with a person's life like you're playing a game of chess."

"I'm not. I'm …"

"So, you didn't send Tobias here to whisk me away from Everlast … from my home of twenty-two years?"

"Yes, of course, I did."

I pinched the bridge of my nose. "In an effort to keep my brain from exploding, can you please elaborate?"

"I love you."

"You don't even know me."

"Yes, I do. From the moment I met you, I knew you were the one."

"The one you plan on driving insane?"

"The one that's meant for me," he corrected.

"Are you high?" I asked. "Can vampires even get high?"

"I have been high since the moment I laid eyes on you."

I rested my head on the nearest wood paneled wall and then banged it against it. "Is everyone in this town psychotic?"

"Sapphire, please calm down."

"Calm down?" I asked incredulously. "I just found out that two of the vampires I trusted most in this world have been pulling my strings like I'm some sort of puppet!"

"You can still trust me," he promised.

"The hell! You haven't even told me why you did this!"

"I didn't want to eat you!" he roared, fed up with my verbal assault. "I cared enough about you to try to get you away from me."

"And it had nothing to do with my house and land being in your way?"

"Sapphire, the hovel that I was raised in was a third of the size of your house, and I would have died before I let someone tear it down to make way for progress. As much as the community pressured me, I never intended to force your hand. That's why I tried to appeal to your reason on the occasions that we spoke about it."

"Appeal to my reason? You mean, talk some sense into me?"

"What are you on about?"

"You know exactly what I'm on about! Every single time you spoke to me before the other night, you actually said the words 'talk some sense into you' right before you'd tell me how my absence is essential to a harmonious vampire community. Don't get all high and mighty now."

"But I …"

"Shut up. You don't get to talk to me anymore. I want you to leave me alone. Don't call me, don't send me texts, don't even send up smoke signals. Unless you find out who's been lurking around my house, I don't want to speak to you. We can live in the same town without speaking." I turned to leave. "We've already proven that."

"Sapphire, please."

I stopped but didn't look at him. I couldn't look at those distraught green eyes for one more second. I was afraid I'd lose my nerve. "Just don't. You've done enough."

"Okay," he conceded. "But only for the time being. I want you to consider forgiving me for this. Not because of my feelings for you, but because I truly am sorry for what I've done. I had no idea things would turn out this way."

"No idea at all?"

"Sapphire, let me finish."

I crossed my arms. "Fine."

"When I called Tobias and asked him to come, I was desperate. I didn't think I had another choice. Separating lust and hunger when I'm around you has been … hard—nearly impossible. You make me weak, Sapphire. I am not in a position to be weak."

As I listened to what had to be the most insane apology in the history of apologies, I actually pitied Kieran. I had zero doubt that he was telling me the truth, and that was just sad. "Kieran …" I trailed off as I turned to look into his eyes. "I forgive you for what you did, and I even understand why you did it, but you have to understand that I am going to be mad at both you and Tobias for a very, very long time. You can't sorry your way out of my anger."

"I understand, a rúnsearc."

I held a hand up. "Secret's out, Kieran, remember?"

"I remember," he said bitterly. "I will never forget."

"Never is a long time." I pursed my lips. I didn't want to feel sorry for him after what he'd done, but I did. "Doubly so in your world."

He held his hand out. "Friends then?"

I put my hand in his. "How about friends, twice removed?"

Examining our intertwined hands, he asked, "If I would have done this right, would you have given me a chance?"

"You already know the answer to that," I said, sighing as I slipped my hand from his light grip. "But all that's changed now. I may forgive you, but you still betrayed me. I won't forget that—ever."

With an earnest expression, he said, "I can't give you up. I can't. You're as rare as hen's teeth, Sapphire. You're irreplaceable."

Confused, I shook my head. "As rare as … what?"

"What I mean is that it is rare to find someone that will be compatible with you over several long lifetimes. It's nearly impossible. I can't live with myself, knowing that I've done this to you … that I've ruined my chance at happiness because I was afraid to trust myself."

"I think I've reached my quota of love declarations today, Kieran, and I've got to go. I'll see you around."

He followed me to the door. He didn't seem to be angry, just defeated. "That's it?

"That's it." I knew he'd hear how my heart pounded. I didn't care. I had to do it this way, or I would let him talk me into something I wasn't ready for … something like genuine forgiveness. When I came here, I hoped he would tell me that he'd done this out of hatred or spite, not love. That made things infinitely harder because as hard as I tried not to see it, I wasn't blind to the fact that Kieran was an incredibly decent man.

"I understand."

I waited until I was almost out of his gate before I whispered, "Goodbye, Kieran." There was no doubt in my mind that I'd never be on a first name basis with him again.

ALL I WANT FOR CHRISTMAS ARE MY TWO FRONT FANGS

***

It wasn't until I stepped onto the sidewalk in front of Kieran's house that everything hit me. I had just been epically screwed. What both of them had done was downright despicable, and here I was making excuses for them. No. Hell no! It was time I grow a proverbial pair and get what I came here after—payback. It wasn't fair that they had so much power over me. From now on, I would have the power, and little by little, I would exact my revenge on them ... as soon as I figured out what the repercussions of breaking my heart would be.

Hands shaking, I pulled my phone out and sent a text to Korrina and Alexis.

GIRL'S NIGHT 9PM ... YOU IN?

Alexis messaged back immediately.

I'LL BRING THE WINE.

Korrina answered a second later.

I'M IN, GIRL.

Pleased with the way the night was shaping up, I practically skipped my way down the sidewalk. I even smiled up at one the many cameras and gave it a cheeky wink as I went by. Kieran had no idea what was in store for him. Hell hath no fury, right?

***

They say revenge is best served cold for a reason. And that reason is the ice in your heart where the degenerate miscreants that hurt you are concerned. When I got home, I went straight to the DVD cabinet and pulled out Fatal Attraction, Mean Girls, and weirdly, Pulp Fiction. I thought watching Samuel L Jackson shoot people might make me feel better, anything to help me forget about this ultra-shitty day that I was still having trouble processing.

Twenty-four hours ago, I thought I met the vampire love of my life. Now, I was back to square one. I had nothing left to show for me putting myself out there but a broken heart, wounded pride, and an amped-up thirst for punishing wrongdoers. I couldn't wait for Alexis and Korrina to get here. If they couldn't help me cook up a proper plan for retribution, no one could.

An hour or so after dark, Korrina let herself into the house and came into the living room with guns blazing. "Imagine a world where I have to find out that one of my best friends just got fucked over like nobody's business, and I had to hear about it from someone else."

I sighed. Geez, did any news not travel at warp speed in this town? "Who told you?"

"Me," Alexis said from behind her. She was carrying what looked like dry cleaning in one hand and a bottle of tequila in the other. "Ronan told me."

"How much do you know?" I groaned.

"Just that Tobias broke up with you," she said.

"That's it? Un-fucking-believable."

Her eyes widened. "Spill! What else is there?"

"Kieran is Tobias' maker."

"Get out!" Korrina exclaimed. "You're kidding?"

"I wish. Tobias told me Kieran made him come here specifically to lure me away from Everlast because … get this … he's in love with me and didn't want to eat me."

"What? I mean … what? How did Tobias intend to 'lure' you out?"

"Marriage. How else? I wouldn't leave my house for anything less, and even then, it's a stretch."

"And Tobias went along with this?" Alexis asked. "He was okay with marrying you?"

Korrina shook her head. "He never had a choice. The sire

bond is unbreakable. He has to obey him."

"Right. Tobias was really lovely about it. He told me that he would've been happy to marry me, that it wouldn't be a hardship for him, but seriously, what the fuck? Why didn't he tell me from the get-go?"

Alexis handed me the tequila. "Maybe he couldn't? Kieran could have forbidden it. Couldn't he?"

"Yeah, but if that was true, how could he ever have told me at all?"

"You're right, I didn't think about that. Wow. This is crazy."

"Way crazy," I agreed. "Speaking of crazy, why are you guys here so early? I haven't even ordered the pizza yet. And what's with the fancy clothes?"

"Are you shitting me, Saph?" Korrina looked at the small pile of DVDs and the overflowing candy bowl that I'd set out. "You are not doing this. You're going out."

"I wasn't going to sit here and mope," I said defensively. "I was going to plot revenge and stuff."

Korrina's expression was incredulous. "You don't have time for that. You have to get ready."

Alexis handed me her dry cleaning and fluffed out her hair. "Guess what's in the bag. I'll give you a hint. Claire gave it to me."

I put the liquor bottle down on the coffee table and lifted the plastic. "No. Freakin'. Way. Is this what I think it is?"

"It sure is. As soon as I heard what happened, I called Claire, and she put it aside. I had her throw in some blood red underwear as kind of like a 'fuck you' to Tobias. You know, it's like saying, 'I'm going to let another man take off this dress, and that lucky bastard is going to find this underneath'."

"Okay," I said, laughing. "You've already thought this out,

haven't you?"

"Girl, this is bullshit. If you want revenge, the best way is to show them what they're missing. It will drive them crazy."

"You know," I took the dress off the hanger and held the mostly see-through lace up to my body. "This might be just deliciously evil enough to work." I grinned. "So, tell me … where are we going?"

Several shots of tequila later, I was almost ready to go dancing. I wasn't exactly on board with Alexis' 'shake your ass and show them what they can't have' idea, but I did plan on having fun tonight. I deserved a good night of debauchery after everything I had been through today.

"Girls!" Korrina called up the stairs. "Let's go!"

Alexis ignored her and continued putting the third coat of mascara on my lashes. "You remember the plan, right? We go in, get a drink, find a table, and then sit back and let the men come to us."

"Wait for the men to come to me. Got it. But, um … when do we turn on the man magnet? Does it need time to warm up, or is it an immediate thing?"

"Don't answer that," Korrina warned from the doorway. "She's just fishing for compliments."

"I don't need your compliments." I spun around in front of the mirror. "Look at this dress on me. It's fantastic!"

"It's such a shame that Tobias turned out to be such a shit," Alexis said, shaking her head sadly as she watched me twirl. "He has great taste, and girl, he is so damn fine."

I grinned at her glazed over look as she thought about Tobias and said, "Down, girl. I know he's ninety-nine percent innocent in this whole thing, but we can't forget that he kept a life-changing secret from me for a week. That makes him as guilty as Kieran."

"Yeah, guilty of being a pussy," Korrina piped in. "I mean, come on, dude. Grow a pair."

"Exactly." I spun around one more time and smiled dizzily. "I don't think it's going to get better than this."

Korrina smiled over my shoulder. "You can't improve upon perfection, sugar."

"Bless your country heart, Korrina."

She winked. "I'm already blessed. Now let's take another shot of courage and say fuck you to those arrogant vampire bastards!"

I smirked at her profanity-laced rant. "Do you kiss Obsidian with that mouth?"

"I kiss him everywhere with this mouth, and I plan on doing it again soon, so let's go. He's waiting."

"He's meeting us? But he hates to go out. On account of that, 'Is it true you turn to mist? Were you really born a vampire? How is it possible for you to eat food?' stuff."

"True, but after promising some very dirty things via text, he agreed to endure the 'true vampire' stuff for the night and to supply protection in case things get ugly."

"And why might things get ugly?

"Kieran is supposed to be there."

"Kieran is going to a dance club called The Cheshire Cat? No way. That shit just happens in the Twilight Zone. Does he even own regular clothes?"

"Yes, he does, and he can really fill out a pair of jeans," Alexis supplied. "By the way, I don't believe we've heard the specific details of what's in those jeans yet. Why is that?"

I laughed. "Uh, because you're both married?"

"Married-smarried. If Ronan looked that hot in jeans, I'd talk about his assets, too."

"His ass does look that good," Korrina disagreed. "That man is sex personified."

"That man is acting like a damn psycho. You should have seen the way he acted when he found out about Tobias breaking up with Sapphire. I'm honestly not sure if I want him to come to meet us tonight."

"Oh, he'll simmer down when he sees Sapphire bringing the male population to their knees with the way she looks in that dress."

I studied my friends as they gave each other a meaningful look. Those witches were brewing up something secret. "What? What did you two do?"

"We polled the town," Alex said, bouncing on her feet with excitement. "Well, not the whole town, but most of the men that we walked by on the way here."

"You polled them?"

"Yeah, and you rate a consistent eight or nine out of ten with every guy we asked. Some thought you lost a point or two because you aren't a vampire, or because you're a female, and one thought you were too tall, but overall, you're pretty admired by the town and a pretty hot commodity, now that people have seen you with Tobias, Kieran, and Obsidian."

"Wait a minute. Are you being serious? Did you guys really ask about me on the street?"

"Are you mad?" Korrina asked, looking as sheepish as a nymph could.

"Depends," I told her. "Did you get any of their numbers?"

"Atta girl!" Alexis cried. "If we don't have a vampire in love with you by Christmas, I'll eat my shoe."

"That's completely unnecessary."

"Says you," she told me with a wink. "Let's go make Kieran feel like an idiot."

CHAPTER NINE

The Cheshire Cat was a small building in the center of town, and by all appearances, it was empty. There was no sign of life, no noise, or even cars parked out front. "Are you guys sure this is it?" I asked. "We're not about to walk into an opium den, are we?"

Korrina laughed. "An opium den? In Everlast?"

"You never know."

Alexis walked to a discreet door that almost blended into the stucco wall. "I think this is it. Ready?"

"Yeah." I straightened the skirt of my dress. "I'm ready."

We walked single file into the club, then stood together to take in the scene. It was positively swarming with vampires, and every single one of them stopped what they were doing when we stepped in the door.

I turned to the girls. "Well, at least this isn't awkward. Let's get a drink."

"Let the other beauties get the drinks," a deep voice whispered into my ear, a moment before an arm wrapped around my waist. "I believe I was promised a dance."

"Okay," I said to Obsidian. "But I don't do the Macarena."

He spun me around to face him and gave me a wickedly sexy smile. "Then we already have something in common. I can't say I'm surprised. You are the perfect woman."

"Wow, you're laying it on pretty thick tonight. What did Korrina promise to do to you?"

"Many, many dirty things." He twirled me around and then brought me back close to him as we swayed to the music. "I'm going for extra brownie points. How do you think I'm doing?"

"Very smooth," I told him, trying to look graceful as I

struggled to match his movements. "Very Patrick Swayze."

"That is praise indeed. Korrina has a thing for Dirty Dancing."

"Gee, I wonder why."

"I believe it's the sexual energy," he said unnecessarily. "I think it turns her on."

"She's a nymph. Used dryer sheets probably turn her on."

He looked thoughtful. "I'm not sure, though we have had sex on the dryer more than once."

I looked toward the heavens. "TMI, Obsidian, TMI."

His rich laughter made the hairs on the back of my neck stand up. "Sorry, I am nothing, if not a slave to my wife's desires."

"That's nice, but I'm telling you now if you try to lift me like a bird at the end of this song, I'm leaving."

"I'm fairly certain that I can control myself," he said chuckling.

I nodded curtly. "See that you do."

When the song was over, Obsidian led me to a darkened booth on the outskirts of the room to sit with Alexis then led his wife onto the floor. I had to admire the pair as I took a sip of the gigantic Long Island iced tea Alexis shoved in front of me as soon as I sat down. They were both so attractive, and even more so when they were together.

"Wow. Look at those two," Alexis said, echoing my thoughts aloud. "They are so perfect together."

"Yeah, but so are you and Ronan," I countered.

She took a long draw from the straw in her pink, frothy drink. "I'm not so sure."

I turned away from the Raines' perfection to glare at her. "Spill it, lady."

"Ronan ... he seems changed. He yells at me all the time and disappears for hours without telling me where he's going."

"Do you think he has someone on the side?"

"I don't think so. We're having more sex than we ever have. It's not romantic sex, but it's sex nonetheless."

"Are you sure we're talking about the same Ronan ... black hair, dark eyes, talks like a leprechaun?"

"Yep, same guy."

"Has he ever acted like this before?"

"Never. It's weird. You'll see when he gets here. Everyone is noticing a change in his personality."

"Well, it looks like I'll get my chance," I said, waving at the Irishman at the door. "There he is."

Ronan looked his usual, cheerful self as he kissed Alexis and me on the cheek then sat down to join us. "So, ladies, how's the revenge plan going?"

"So far, so good," I told him when Alexis stayed silent. "I plan on stealing Obsidian away from Korrina when she's not looking. He's an excellent dancer."

"As good as me?" he asked.

"I don't know, Ronan. You've never asked me to dance before."

"That cannot be true." He stood and helped me from the booth before speaking to his wife. "Can you get me a Guinness, Alex?"

"S-sure," she said, obviously crushed. "Bottle or pint?"

"A pint, love."

"Okay."

I tried to catch Alexis' eye as she walked to the bar, but she never looked up from the floor. She was right. Ronan was acting weird, and it was hurting her.

"Ronan," I admonished. "That was rude. You barely said hello to her then sent her to fetch you a beer."

"How was it rude?" he asked, offended at the accusation.

"I just told you. You treated her like your favorite maid."

"She's fine," he assured me, pulling me so close to his body, I could smell his shampoo. "We're here for revenge, right?"

"I guess." I wasn't exactly comfortable with the odd look in his eyes.

We swayed to the music for a minute or so before he spoke softly into my ear. "Kieran told me what happened."

My step faltered. "He did?"

"Yes. You should have listened to me about Tobias. I told you he would break your heart."

Wasn't that the painful truth? Acting weird or not, Ronan had hit that one right on the head. "Yeah, I probably should have."

"I could kill him for what he's done to you," he growled angrily. "To you! Who is he to think that you aren't good enough? You're beautiful, sexy … especially in this dress. And smart, you're so smart! What man wouldn't want you?"

"I am pretty awesome," I joked. "I can't believe I'm still single."

"If I were unmarried, I would marry you in a heartbeat," he murmured, and then he kissed my neck in a decidedly non-friendly way … if there was a friendly way to kiss someone's neck.

Frozen with shock, I said, "Ronan, Alexis is my friend. I would appreciate it if you didn't do that again."

"Don't worry. He won't be doing that again," Alexis told me. I turned to find her fuming, looking like she was ready to murder her husband. "How could you, Ronan?"

"Don't overreact, a stóirín. You're making a scene."

"A scene? A fucking scene! You're trying to make out with my best friend in front of every vampire we know!"

"I'm going to go," I muttered, backing away from the two before running back to my drink like it could save me from the wraith Alexis was about to lay down.

"What the hell is going on?" Korrina asked as she and Obsidian slid into the booth after me. "Alexis and Ronan look like they are going to come to blows out there."

"He kissed my neck while we were dancing and said he would marry me if he were single."

"He didn't!" Obsidian exclaimed, looking back to the dance floor and frowning when he saw that the pair had vanished. "I'll go make sure that he behaves himself. See you two in a bit." He kissed us both on the cheek and sprinted out the door.

I stared after him. "I'm worried, Korrina."

She frowned. "Me, too. It looks like it might be splitsville for those two."

"This is insane. Why is almost every single vampire I'm close to so into me all of a sudden? Even Tobias, who was brought here against his will, said he'd marry me. It's freakin' weird!"

"Totally weird. Stay away from Obsidian, okay?"

I laughed. "You got it, chick."

Korrina gathered her wrap and purse. "I guess we should get out of here before you break up another semi-happy couple."

"Yeah," I agreed, looking at the vampires giving me the 'you're a home wrecker' look. "Are you still up for tequila and movies at my house?"

"Of course! Just let me check on Obsidian, and I'll come right over."

ALL I WANT FOR CHRISTMAS ARE MY TWO FRONT FANGS

"Okay, see ya soon."

***

As I nervously began to walk the four blocks back to my house alone, I used the time to go over the night's events. It was either that or run like a crazy person in heels to my house. I was terrified to be by myself, regardless of the early hour. For the first time since those unforgettable first three weeks of the great vampire move-in, I was terrified.

I didn't think anything could be worse than this whole stalker thing, but the thought of losing my best friend was so much worse. Alexis had to be devastated by what Ronan did. And though it seemed like she overheard me tell him to back off, she could be angry at me for being an unwilling victim. I'd seen her get completely irate over way less of an offense. No, there would definitely be no peace in my mind until I heard her say that she wasn't mad.

"Hey," a familiar voice called from behind me. "Can I walk with you?"

I stopped to wait on Tobias and closed my eyes while I counted to ten. Of course, he would show up right now. "I guess so."

He fell into step with me on the opposite side of the sidewalk. "I heard what happened at the club."

"What the hell is with this town? Already? Does everyone know?"

"Pretty much the whole town. They also know that we broke up. According to the rumor Kieran is circulating, I broke things off with you."

"What did Kieran really say? Was he pissed that you told me about the sire thing?"

"Furious, but only at himself."

"Good," I said, more relieved than I thought I'd be.

"Good?"

"Well, yeah. One, because he's mad at himself, as he should be, and two, he didn't kick your ass for being truthful."

The reflection of the Christmas lights on the house next to Tobias made his eyes look intensely blue as he grinned at me. "No, there was no ass-kicking. However, there was a tongue lashing because I didn't warn him that you knew his secret. Oh, and he forbade me to get within four feet of you."

"You're kidding?" I stopped walking. "Try it."

"It's impossible."

Huffing with irritation, I lunged for his hand and was amused to see him snatch it away like I touched him with a branding iron.

"I told you," he said. "I can't touch you."

"Why did he do that?"

He arched a honey-blond eyebrow. "Why do you think? He doesn't want the competition."

"He doesn't have competition," I said, shaking my head.

"No?"

"No. I don't want either one of you."

"Ouch!" he said, clutching his heart.

"Can you blame me?"

"Not at all. I expected it. Honestly, with Kieran who he is to me, I doubt it would've worked out between us, anyway. A centuries-old vampire isn't going to forget someone they think is their soul mate."

"Do you think it will ever work out? Do you think he will ever let you have a life of your own?"

He smiled and raised his hand as if he wanted to touch my

face then thought better of it. "If you had been any other woman on this planet, I think he would have given his blessing. He's not a monster, Saphir."

"Did he tell you to tell me that?"

"No."

"Did he tell you to tell me that?" I parroted.

"Saphir!"

I giggled and continued walking. "You're right. It wouldn't work out between us. I'd probably always wonder if it was real."

"I respect women. I would have treated you like a queen, whether I liked you or not."

"What a gentleman," I muttered sarcastically.

"Don't take that the wrong way, Saphir. I'm just as smitten with you as everyone else seems to be. There's an excellent reason for that, by the way."

"Is it because I'm B negative?"

He rolled his eyes. "No. It's because you're genuine. You're you. I hope that never changes."

I stared up at the full moon above us and smiled. "How could it? I'm me."

"Once you become a vampire, you might change more than you think."

"Who says I'll become a vampire?"

"I do. I'll sire you myself if I have to."

"Not if that means Kieran will be able to tell me what to do, you won't. He'd be able to, wouldn't he?"

"He could order me to tell you to do something," he admitted with reluctance.

"Something like live happily ever after with him?"

"Something exactly like that."

"No, thanks."

He smiled approvingly. "I understand, but the offer still stands if you ever have need of me."

"Thanks. I appreciate it."

After walking the last block to our houses in silence, I asked Tobias the question that had been on my mind since he told me that his arrival in Everlast was planned. "Are you going to go back to Canada?"

He looked down to the sidewalk before he spoke. "I fly to Saint John tomorrow night to secure housing. I'll be back in a couple days to start packing."

"Oh … well, have a nice life, I guess?"

"Saphir, you can't get rid of me that easily. I'll come back to visit. We didn't get a chance to watch the movies I wanted to show you. I haven't forgotten."

"Nor have I."

"Good. Shall I walk you to your door?"

I waved away his gentlemanly concern. "No. I can take care of myself."

"I have no doubt of that, Saphir." He smiled and spread his arms wide. "I would hug you if I could."

"I know you would, and I love you for it, but let's skip it until I can convince Kieran to let you near me."

"That might be best. Are you sure I can't walk you to the door?"

I glanced at the dark front window then took a long last look at everything that made him special to me—the shape of his face, the way he stood, the smile that never quite left his lips—all of it, and I knew I would miss him terribly. I really hoped he was telling the truth when he said he would visit. If anything, I wanted to be his friend. "No, I'm all right, Tobias. Have a safe trip tomorrow."

"I will. Good night, Saphir."

"Good night, Mr. Faust."

I started up the driveway and was almost to the front porch when I heard Tobias walking behind me. "Kieran is Ronan's maker, too," he said. "I thought you ought to know since you're friends with him … under normal circumstances."

"Great! That's super awesome!" I said brightly, sarcasm dripping from my words. "Anything else I need to know?"

He smiled. "Yes. That dress looks amazing on you."

Laughing, I twirled around, letting the layers of the dress swish around me. "It does, doesn't it? A friend with great taste thought of me when he saw it in the store. Thanks for that, by the way, and thanks for telling me about Ronan."

He bowed. "It's my pleasure, Saphir. Good night."

"Good night."

With a bemused grin, I watched Tobias until his front door closed, then I climbed the stairs to my porch, dug out my keys, and promptly dropped them. The loud jingle of my key ring crashing to the porch punctuated how deserted the neighborhood was at this time of night. It was almost spooky.

"Quiet as the grave," I muttered as I picked up the keys then shrieked when my phone meowed at me. Breathing heavily, I pulled it out of my pocket and glanced at the screen.

ALEXIS IS OKAY, BUT WE HAVE TO POSTPONE. SORRY.

Relieved to hear good news from Korrina, I let out a deep sigh and typed.

GOOD. SEE YOU TOMORROW.

But my elation didn't last long. The moment I put my phone

back in my pocket, the happiness faded away to reveal the underlying fear I was feeling before. And something seemed off … like I was being watched by someone. Someone that was very good at hiding around my house. Maybe it was just my mind working overtime, but I wasn't going to take any chances. I knew that Tobias had gotten inside the house somehow, so it stood to reason that another vampire could. What if he was in there waiting on me?

In complete and total irritation, I realized what I'd have to do and quickly pulled out my phone to type out the quickest text I'd ever sent, the whole time wondering how the hell Kieran, of all people, had become my last resort.

CAN YOU PICK ME UP AT MY HOUSE?

His answer was immediate.

THREE MINUTES.

"Thank you, God," I breathed out. With Tobias' restrictions and Korrina and Obsidian being occupied with the Seward's problems, I didn't know who else to call, which, frankly, worried me.

***

Kieran was as good as his word, showing up precisely three minutes after the text. I couldn't have been more grateful. I ran to his door before he could even get the car stopped and threw myself in.

"Sapphire!" he complained, holding his chest. "You'll put the heart crossways in me! At least, let me stop the car first!"

"Sorry," I rambled, in a totally panicked but grateful voice. "Those three minutes were the longest of my life! I tried waiting at the end of the steps, but that felt too out in the open. After that, I stood on the end of the porch. That was worse. Finally, I decided that hiding between the hedges and the porch railing was the best choice."

ALL I WANT FOR CHRISTMAS ARE MY TWO FRONT FANGS

His eyes darted around the yard. "I thought I was seeing things when you came out of the bushes. Are you in some kind of trouble?"

"No, just scared out of my ever-loving mind, so thanks for coming. Really, Kieran. Thanks."

"You're welcome, but what has you so afraid?"

I shrugged. "Vampires, I guess? After all the stuff that happened today, and Ronan, and the stalker/spray painter guy, I just didn't want to be alone."

"You haven't forgotten that I'm one of the vampires that hurt you, have you?"

"You wish," I said, glaring at him. "I only called you because I didn't have anyone else to call. And unlike the majority of vampires in this town, you're not scary. Well, not as scary as most of them, anyway."

"No?"

Feeling unnaturally shy, I gave him a small smile. "No. As a matter of fact, I've been thinking about it, and I was wondering if I could sleep at your house tonight. And if that works out, maybe for a few nights? You, my friend, have the safest house in town."

He considered me for a moment. "Is your fear the only reason you're asking?"

"I'm asking because I need a friend. I would ask Obsidian and Korrina, but they're watching over Alexis tonight."

"Of that, I am well aware," he said cryptically. "Do you realize that you have leaves in your hair?" He reached toward me. "May I?"

"Sure." I held myself still while he plucked several evergreen leaves and a small twig from my hair. "How do you know they're watching Alexis?"

"When I was notified of the situation at the Cheshire Cat, I followed them camera by camera until I saw Ronan cause her harm."

"He caused her harm?" I asked, interrupting him. "What happened?"

"I was getting to that."

"Alexis is my best friend. Get to it faster."

He nodded. "Ronan bit her pretty savagely and then hit her when she tried to fight him off. She's okay, but I thought it prudent to take her somewhere he could not follow."

"That fucker!" I spat. "What's being done about this?"

"Korrina and Obsidian are already taking care of things. You know, I'm not one to favor violence being used to punish violence, but Obsidian gave Ronan a well-deserved black eye he won't soon forget before they took Alexis to a safer location. I've brought Ronan back to my house to stay with me until we can get this all straightened out."

I pulled my cell phone from my pocket. "I have to talk to her."

"She doesn't have her phone. I didn't want Ronan to be able to track her with GPS until he's calmed down and they've had a chance resolve things. I asked Korrina to stop at the first place they can find to get her a prepaid cell phone. I give it twenty minutes before she's demanding to speak to you."

"Thirty tops," I told him, feeling a little relieved that Alexis had someone she could trust with her. "Is Ronan at your house now?"

"Yes. He's upset with himself for what he did and very apologetic, but there's something not right with him tonight. I can't have him out there roaming the streets when he's acting so strangely."

"Oh, he's acting strange all right. Did Korrina and Obsidian tell you what he did in the club?"

He grimaced. "He told me himself."

"And did you command him to leave Alexis alone … to leave me alone? You're his sire, right?"

His eyebrows rose. "I am. I told him he was not to harm anyone in this town in any way, himself included."

"Good thinking."

He quirked his lips. "That's why I'm the king."

"Funny," I muttered.

"Are you ready to go? Do you need to get a change of clothes?"

I surveyed my dark house and decided against going in. "Nope. You'll loan me a t-shirt, won't you?"

"Of course," he said, watching me carefully. "You really are afraid to go in there, aren't you?"

"Did you think I called you for an ulterior motive?"

"One can hope."

***

Ronan was waiting on the dimly lit front lawn when we returned to Kieran's house. He walked to my car door and jerked it open, his sudden movements causing me to let out a yip of fear before his maker snapped, "Ronan! Back off!"

"Sapphire," Ronan beseeched, backing away. "Please forgive me for what I did. I don't know what I was thinking."

"Fuck what you did to me!" I yelled, stalking toward him. "What about Alexis?"

"She slapped me. It was a reaction. A bad reaction, I'll admit, but I never intended to hurt her."

"Reaction, huh? A real man doesn't hit a woman, regardless of who started it." I tried not to look at the smug face Kieran was sure

135

to be wearing. "You're a vampire, Ronan. For God's sake, you idiot! You could have really injured her."

He stared at the grass under his feet. "I'm so sorry, Sapphire."

"I'm not the one you need to apologize to," I yelled, my voice verging on hysterical. "You better pray that Alexis will take pity on you and give you the chance to make amends. You certainly don't deserve it after this."

"Sapphire, come with me," Kieran coaxed from where he watched us. "Let me show you to your room."

"You're staying here?" Ronan asked.

"That's none of your fucking business!" I hissed.

Ronan was taken aback by the intensity in my voice and looked almost angry enough to retort, but after a quick glance at his sire, he only nodded and quickly walked past me to go into the house.

When the front door slammed shut, and he was sure Ronan was out of earshot, Kieran attempted to reason with me. "I know you're angry at him. However, I believe he is sorry for what he's done. Alexis will probably forgive him for this. You should try to, as well."

"Maybe she will," I conceded. "But that doesn't make things better or set anything to right."

He put an arm around my shoulders and led me up the steps. "Sapphire, you're feisty when your friends are hurt. Surprisingly feisty."

"Aren't you?"

"I don't think I have enough friends to test the theory."

"Did you send your children to lure them out of town, too?"

He sighed and opened the door. "You're not funny."

"That's a matter of opinion," I told him, grinning at his stiff posture. "So, where am I sleeping?"

"Upstairs, in the room next to mine."

"Really?" I wiggled my eyebrows. "Can I see your bedroom?"

"Why?"

I shrugged. "Because I want to see where the king sleeps."

"Okay, but prepare to be underwhelmed. I spend little time in there."

"I'll find a way to deal with the disappointment," I promised, pointing up the stairs. "Lead the way."

"You are a strange woman, Sapphire."

"Because I want to see your bedroom?"

"Because of that, yes, but mostly because you want to stay here after you found out that I made someone move from Canada to marry you ... and found out that I'm sire to two vampires that have recently hurt you ... and found out that I am jealous enough of your relationship with that tosser, Tobias, that I prohibited him from getting near you. Honestly, I am astounded that you're standing here right now."

He thought he was astounded? No one could be more stupefied by my choice to call Kieran to my rescue than me. And he was right. No sane woman would want to see him again after all that.

"I think it's best if we don't overanalyze what I do, at this point," I decided. "And let's put all that other stuff on the back burner, too. At least until we figure this stalker thing out."

Aiming a thankful smile at me, he said, "You have no idea how delighted I would be to do just that."

"Good."

Kieran beckoned for me to follow him upstairs and led me to the end of the hallway, where he opened the door to a room with dark grey walls, a black-blanketed bed, and not much else. "It's not much to look at, but it's safe, and you can stay as long as you like."

"It's got a bed. That's all I care about. Now quit stalling and let me see your room."

"I'm not stalling, I'm showing you where you're going to sleep during your stay."

"Well, I've seen it." I grabbed him by the arm and excitedly dragged him to the next door. "Open up."

Amused, he begrudgingly consented and unlocked his door. "Okay," he said, stopping me before I could rush into the room. "I'll let you in here, but try to be gentle, a chéadsearc. I am but a simple man."

Hastily nodding, I walked through the door he held open and marveled at what I found, or rather, the one thing I found because there was really only enough space for the triple sized bed that dominated his bedroom.

"Are you serious with this thing?" I asked, shocked at the sheer size of it.

"I realize the size is a bit absurd."

"Don't you mean the cherubs are a bit absurd?" I asked, making a beeline to the intricately carved headboard. "Holy shit, Kieran. I don't know what else to say."

"I realize the cherubs are a bit creepy. It is not something I would choose for myself. It was a gift from the King of Sweden."

I wriggled my eyebrows suggestively. "So, why did the King of Sweden think you needed a bed for fifteen?"

"He wanted to repay me for a favor, and this was all he had to give at the time. He wouldn't take no for an answer. Believe me, I tried."

I walked to the edge of the mattress and ran my fingers along the silk comforter. "How many silkworms had to die to make this blanket?"

"Not one."

"May I?" I asked, gesturing to the bed.

"May you what?"

"Get in your bed."

"Be my guest," He watched me slip off my heels and climb onto the bed before continuing. "Just for the record, you never have to ask to get in my bed."

"Great!" I exclaimed, ignoring his innuendo and diving in toward the middle. I turned over to my back and pretended I was lying in the snow. "I can make silk angels anytime I want!"

Kieran laughed and kneeled on the bed to grab my stocking-covered foot then tugged me under him. "You may be the silliest creature I have ever known."

Blushing as I pushed my dress back into place, I confessed, "I don't know how to take that. You've known a lot of people."

With a slight smile, he nodded thoughtfully. "Yes. Yes, I have."

"Hey! You'd better be nice to me," I warned. "Especially when I'm dangerously close to being able to knee you where it counts."

"Such violence!" he gasped in mock abhorrence.

"Well, you bring out the best in me."

"Yes, I do," he agreed, undressing me with his eyes. "And if I remember correctly, I brought out the best in you … several times."

I shook my head. "You're a dirty old man."

"You're one to talk. Red panties … you vixen."

"Yeah, well, Tobias didn't buy these, so keep your hands to

yourself."

"Oh? You have someone else buying your underwear now?"

"Yep, a real looker. Blonde, blue eyes, great personality, huge rack ... really the whole package."

"You had me going until huge rack part," he admonished. "I think you might be trying to make me jealous."

"No, not now, but I was definitely trying to when I went to the club tonight. The girls heard you were going to be there."

"He had an unavoidable appointment," Ronan said, standing in the open doorway. He was wearing an unreadable expression as he took in the state of things between Kieran and I. "I'm heading home. I'll check in tomorrow."

"Excuse me for a moment," Kieran said apologetically. "Ronan, wait. I need to discuss something with you. Will you meet me in my office?"

Ronan nodded. "Of course."

Kieran stood and helped me up. "Feel free to roam around or stay in here. There's a TV and remote in the armoire if you get bored."

"Okay, but before you go, do you have any shaving cream, or maybe, a Sharpie?"

"Why?"

"No reason," I said, feigning innocence.

He kissed my forehead. "Just try to behave yourself while I'm gone, will you?"

"I'll give it a shot," I called after him. "But I make no promises."

Kieran left the room hopeful and amused, while I was left wondering what I was doing letting him charm me again. And why I really, really wanted him to.

ALL I WANT FOR CHRISTMAS ARE MY TWO FRONT FANGS

CHAPTER TEN

After five minutes alone in Kieran's bedroom, I gave up on waiting for Alexis to call or him to come back and opened up the armoire. Just like he said I would, I found a TV and remote inside. With the remote in tow, I climbed back onto the bed and got comfortable by slipping off my thigh high hose and nestling under the silky blanket. It was heaven, and I was still giving serious thought to what I would have to do for a king to get my own fifteen person bed when Kieran finally returned.

"I see you made yourself comfortable," he said, eyeing my discarded stockings on the edge of the bed as he closed the door.

"Yep, and thanks a lot for letting me get used to this bed. Now I need to find a king to sleep with to get one of my own."

"That wasn't the kind of favor I was referring to, Sapphire. I draw the line at sleeping with men for furniture."

"If you say so," I told him, smirking at his distressed expression.

"You do realize that most vampires aren't as … ambiguous as we're portrayed in books and on television, don't you?"

"Yes, but I didn't want to judge, just in case."

His eyes opened wide. "Sapphire! I didn't sleep with anyone for this bed. I've never even had sex in this bed."

I threw my hands up in mock exasperation. "Great. Now I have to have sex with you here."

"And I will be happy to oblige you, but it will have to wait. It's getting late, and I believe I'll need to run an errand soon."

"You believe you will? Where do you think that you'll be going?"

"That depends on you. Where did you find the bottle of blood that you brought to Tobias as a housewarming gift?"

"At the Target in Lynchburg."

He checked his watch. "Good. We have a little time before they close. Ever since Tobias shared the bottle with me, I can't get it out of my mind," he explained. "It was a favorite of mine when I lived in Germany."

"Then I'm glad I found it."

"As am I. Would you care to accompany me?"

I narrowed my eyes. "Are you trying to distract me from worrying about Alexis?"

"Yes. Is it working?"

"Let me see ... go to Target with a vampire elder or sit here and worry?" I clicked off the TV and unburied myself from the covers. "Hell yes, it's working! Sign me up! It'll be like watching a nature show on National Geographic. A vampire in its natural habitat ... fascinating."

He frowned. "I can assure you, it's not."

I shook my head. "Nope. You're not going to convince me of that until I see it myself."

"Very well." He picked up the hose. "Do you want to put these on before we go?"

"Do you think I need to?"

"Again, that depends on you. Will you let me watch you put them on?"

I slid off the bed and snatched them from his hand. "Again, you wish."

He smirked. "How well you know me already."

***

"Look how he chooses the best basket before shopping," I said, in a loud, terrible British accent. *"Not many people realize that vampires are some of the pickiest creatures on Earth, sometimes to their detriment."*

Kieran stopped walking, and I narrowly avoided running into him and a display of furniture polish. "Are you finished?" he asked.

"Almost."

He sighed. "Proceed."

"The vampire has keen senses," I continued, now holding up an imaginary camera as I stalked a few steps behind him. *"They use all the subtle nuances and scents from their environment in their search for food. Notice how the vampire uses the hanging sign to direct his path."*

A bemused associate approached us as I finished my spiel. "Can I help you find anything?"

"Unless you stock sanity, I don't think you can," Kieran told her. "But thank you."

"See how the centuries have cultured the vampire into becoming a smooth conversationalist," I resumed, getting louder and louder the farther we got away from the red-shirted employee.

Kieran smiled awkwardly at a few customers nearby and put his arm around me as we rounded the vampire aisle. "I don't remember you being so ... spirited the last time I took you somewhere."

"Well, that was before I knew you tried to ruin my life. You get crazy Sapphire from here on out. Just feel lucky you aren't getting angry Sapphire."

"Trust me, I am." He surveyed the refrigerated sectioned before asking, "Where did you find the *Schokolade Herzblut*?"

"In the middle. On the bottom row."

Spying the silver label, he strode purposely to the bottles and started filling his basket. "Is there anything you need while we're here?" He straightened when the basket couldn't hold another bottle. "Pajamas, perhaps?"

I shrugged and said, "I guess," though I didn't think I'd be needing them. At this point, I wasn't going to try to kid myself into thinking that I wouldn't sleep with Kieran tonight. As insane as it was, something in me wanted to give him another shot.

Kieran set his basket of blood on a display table and waded into the racks with me when we finally made it across the store to women's sleepwear. "How about something like this?" he asked, holding up a long white flannel nightgown covered with pale pink roses.

"Should I save it until I'm old enough to wear it?" I asked, horrified by his decision.

"Too old-fashioned?"

"You think?"

"I honestly don't know. The last time a woman spent the night in my bed, this is what she wore."

"That's just sad," I said, flipping through a rack and producing a short and silky black nightgown. "I think I'll match your bed in this."

He looked up from the circular rack of Santa Claus themed nightgowns that he was flipping through. "I believe you will. Does that mean you'll be testing the theory tonight?"

"Yes, it does. Unless you think there's no room for me."

"I believe I could spare a little room," he said, joining me at my rack and tucking my hair behind my ears. "It might be a tight squeeze, but we'll make do."

I raised my eyebrows at his double entendre. "Are we still talking about the bed?"

"Were we ever?"

"Not on my end," I admitted, then grabbed a size small and waded out of the sea of pajamas, leaving Kieran behind. I waited in the aisle as he picked up the basket that was literally groaning from the weight of the eight bottles of blood he'd shoved in it, and we began the long walk to the checkout.

"Anything else you'd like to add before we go?" he asked.

"Now that you mention it." I took out my imaginary camera and regained the horrible accent I had before. *"Contrary to popular belief, vampires can't use the glamouring ability for blood, whether fresh or bottled. Observe as the vampire uses a debit card to make his purchases, just like the rest of the mundanes."*

Kieran pinched the bridge of his nose. "Sapphire, honestly."

I ignored him in favor of giving the associate at the checkout a huge grin and bursting out with, *"Vampires ... fascinating creatures of the night or mindless, blood-thirsty monsters? Find out Thursday 8/7 Central on the National Geographic Channel."*

The second the transaction was done, Kieran grabbed the receipt and bags with a curt nod and started walking away, nearly jogging in a bid to get away from me.

Giggling at his exasperation, I stalked behind him and shouted, "And ... CUT!" as he walked out of the automatic doors.

As soon as we got back to his house, Kieran showed me into a gleaming stainless-steel wonderland of a kitchen that was utterly wasted on a vampire and flicked on the light to put away the two week supply of blood he'd bought. "Feel free to make yourself a drink," he said. "I just have a few things to take care of before I'm all yours."

"Thanks." I smiled appreciatively. "Where can I find the glasses?"

"In the press."

I cocked my head to the side. "Try me again? This time, pretend I'm American."

"The cabinet, a chéadsearc," he said, laughing. "My apologies."

Following his eyes, I walked to the cabinet and pulled out a glass. Can I get you anything?"

"Sure." He nodded at the bottle of Jameson on the counter. "You know what I like."

With a smirk, I turned around and leaned against the counter. "Yep. I sure do. Let's see … there's being in control, having your d—"

"That'll do, Sapphire," he said hurriedly.

"I can keep going."

He grinned. "I'm quite sure you can."

Still smiling, Kieran left for his office, and I went to work pouring him a double of whiskey and a glass of the newly acquired blood. He had to be anxious to have a taste of it now that he had it here, and if we were going to be in each other's lives as friends or more, I needed to show him the same courtesy he shows me when I eat, even if it totally grosses me out.

"Okay," I said, balancing the glasses on a tray as I used my free hand and hip to open Kieran's office door. "I brought you whiskey and blood. I wasn't sure which you'd prefer."

He looked up from his iPad and smiled. "That's perfect. Thank you."

"You're welcome." I sat down in the cushy leather recliner opposite of his desk. "Don't let me bother you. I'm just going to watch you work for a while."

"You're not a bother. I wanted to ask you something, anyway."

I kicked off my shoes and tucked my feet beneath me. "Shoot."

"I've secured the acquisition of the adjacent twenty-five thousand acres north of Everlast. What do you think of that?"

I took a sip of the whiskey I'd poured for myself and thought for a second before answering. "I think expansion is a smart move that will require minimal effort on your part. It's flat land. There's no natural springs or creeks. Besides building more houses, you'll only have to establish the same kind of retailers you have on the south side and petition the USPS to move to a more central location for it to be convenient for everyone."

"Then you think it's a good idea?"

"Yes, but the humans won't thank you for it."

"Well, there is more than one way to chase a devil around a stump, Sapphire."

"And that is?"

"I'm inviting them to live here—humans, weres, elves, nymphs, even satyrs. It seems wrong to exclude a race because it's different than mine. It's an elitist attitude that I shouldn't promote among the vampires in my region."

"The vampires are going to be pissed," I pointed out. "Really pissed."

"They'll get over it," he assured me, taking a sip of blood then lisping through his fangs, "They have no other choice in the matter. They can protest, and spy and spray paint all they want. I have the right to do what's best for the community."

"No doubt a brilliant businessman dreamed up a provision spelling that out in their HOA contracts," I said, complimenting him on his sneakiness. He was a freakin' ninja at hiding his ulterior motives … and he always had ulterior motives.

He shook his head. "You flatter me, but I was just protecting my own interests when I did it. There was nothing benevolent about it."

I sat back, dejected. "Yeah, I'm trying to get used to that."

"Get used to what?"

"To you. You only do things that benefit you."

Draining his glass in one long swallow, he set it down and slurred, "I used to do things only for myself until I met a beautiful and very angry young woman. She stole my heart."

I pointed to myself. "Me?"

"Who else?"

"How should I know? You don't get to be centuries old without loving a few women."

He raised an eyebrow. "Loving?"

"Take that however you like," I told him and felt my cheeks fill with color.

"Sapphire, I have only 'loved' a handful of women in my long life, and all of them were my wives."

"Except for me," I noted.

"Except for you," he agreed.

"Wow. I got the honor of being your first sin-filled romp. How did I get so fortunate?"

"You were repulsed by me. I could barely get you to stay in the same room, much less, marry me."

I sat up straight. "I have never been repulsed by you, Kieran. I wish I were, but I'm not."

He was skeptical. "You're not?"

"I'm here, aren't I? I called you tonight. Oh, and I didn't knee you in the balls when I really should have, especially after all the shitty things I'd just found out about." I paused in thought. "Personally, I think you have some kind of unnatural charisma that makes you impossible to hate."

His eyes glowed amber in the firelight as he stared at me. "You are all kindness, Sapphire."

Standing up for a refill, I took his empty glass. "Aren't I?"

A full two minutes passed before Kieran joined me in the kitchen and finally semi-answered my question. "You are more than I deserve."

I shivered as he swept the hair away from my neck and kissed me between it and my shoulder blade. "I am?"

"You are."

I finished rinsing out the glass of blood and dried my hands before I turned around to face his intense green gaze. "See, that just proves my point. When you say sweet things like that, you make it so difficult for me to hate you."

He stepped closer and put his hands on my waist. "I apologize. I'll try harder."

"Harder?" I asked, arching an eyebrow.

The next few seconds were a blur. Meeting his lunge for me halfway, our mouths collided in a desperate kiss that would have made both of us gasp for air if he needed to breathe. Mindless with want, I spent several seconds on the frenzied unbuttoning of his shirt and pants, then he took control. With his quick, precise movements, his hands seemed to be everywhere at once, pulling my dress over my head, dragging my panties to my ankles, and pushing me into position over the granite countertop. He guided his thumbs along my spine, then spread his fingers out to run his palms down from the side of my breasts to my hips.

"Sapphire, you are so fecking beautiful."

ALL I WANT FOR CHRISTMAS ARE MY TWO FRONT FANGS

I closed my eyes, threw my head back, and moaned, the anticipation of him pushing inside of me almost too much to take. Kieran brought out a hunger in me that could never be duplicated with anyone else, including Tobias, and as he thrust himself inside me from behind, stretching me until I was filled, I knew I'd never want anyone else—ever. There was a time when that thought would have terrified me. Now it was my only foreseeable future, and I was absolutely fine with that.

Kieran molded his firm chest to my back and laced his fingers with mine. "I have to know, a chéadsearc," he whispered, moving at an achingly slow pace. "Do I have any hope of making you my wife, or is this all we will ever share?"

Time seemed to stand still for me after he spoke. Did I just hear Kieran ask me to be his wife? Was he kidding? He had to be kidding, right?

"Sapphire?" he asked, stilling within me.

"Can we stop for a minute?"

"Of course," he said, immediately allowing me to face him.

"Kieran, I...." I looked him over as I tried to find the words for what I was feeling. His cheeks were tinged pink below predatory eyes. He was focused like I'd never seen him before. He wanted me. I could practically feel it radiating from him. But it didn't scare me. If anything, it encouraged me to accept him. Who else would ever want me like this? And really, how often does something like this happen to a person? I mean, there had to be a reason why people use the expression, 'once in a lifetime', right?

Suddenly realizing I was having difficulty expressing myself, he leaned down to kiss me with a slight smile. "Do not worry. I won't push you into anything you're not ready for."

"It's not that. It's just I know that I shouldn't marry you. It's insane after everything you did, but Kieran, this feels real. When Tobias asked me to marry him, I felt a thrill of happiness; that's it. This is different. This is ... a freakin' out of body experience. And it's not just sexual." I smirked. "Though, the sex is exemplary. I guess what I'm saying is that I actually feel something for you … besides the usual anger."

"The usual anger?" he asked.

"Yeah, you know, about the house. It was unfair for me to be upset with you for wanting a haven for your vampires. Everyone should have a place where they can be themselves."

"That is why I gave you the job," Kieran told me, smiling widely. "You have a conscience. You have empathy for a race that is vastly different from yours. Everlast needs someone like you."

"Don't interrupt me," I scolded.

"Then tell me your answer, woman! Are you saying yes to me? I cannot bear the wait."

"I'm saying, yes," I confirmed, trying to hold back a wide grin of my own.

He looked to the ceiling and closed his eyes for a brief moment. I wasn't sure if it was out of relief or whether he was sending up a quick prayer of thanks—or both.

"You okay over there?" I asked.

His green eyes had turned to amber when he lifted his lids. Grinning, he lifted me to the counter and settled between my thighs. "Don't toy with me, my love. If you say yes to me. You will be mine forever." He paused awkwardly. "That did not come out right."

"I know what you meant," I said, moaning as he moved into me without warning. "I won't change my mind."

"I love you," Kieran whispered, before taking my mouth with his and kissing me until I couldn't think.

"OH MY GOD!" a woman's voice screeched.

In a flash, Kieran had me picked up and turned away from the woman I'd seen on the stairs earlier in the evening. Wrapping my legs around his waist to hold on, I glared at him and asked, "You're not going to tell me that you're already married, are you?"

"Gross," the woman said. She threw my dress over his shoulder. "Let her get dressed, Kieran, and put some damn pants on! How long do I have to look at your backside?"

Sighing, he let me slide to my feet and handed me the dress. "I apologize. I should have made sure we were in private."

I slipped the dress over my head and straightened it into place. "It's okay. I wasn't exactly fighting you off."

"The pants, Kieran!" the woman yelled, barely holding back laughter as she covered her eyes.

"Two minutes," he whispered. "I'll get her out of here, and we'll—"

"Go make silk angels?" I interrupted, giving him a more than a friendly peck on the lips.

He grinned and returned the kiss with interest. "Until daylight," he promised. "I'll meet you there.

CHAPTER ELEVEN

As I ran up the stairs like a giddy school girl, everything kind of dawned on me. I was engaged to Kieran Kinane ... me ... a human woman was engaged to a regional vampire leader. This was unprecedented, as was the new community Kieran was thinking of building. I had a feeling we would be making plenty of waves in the vampire's notoriously calm pond in doing both of those things. That was a scary undertaking for me, especially in my fragile state, but ultimately, I knew it was a necessary one. It was only a matter of time before someone sued one of the regions for discrimination. If I had been born with a sizable trust fund, it probably would have been me that filed the first lawsuit.

Putting all of my worries aside until later, I hurried into the bathroom to get a look at myself. What I saw in the mirror was something I hadn't seen in a long time—the image of a happy woman. After the death of my grandparents, I had nothing to look forward to at the end of the day and no one to come home to. Even as good of a friend as Alexis was, I'd felt adrift without a loved one to share my life. I didn't feel that way anymore. Finally, I felt whole.

"Sapphire?" Kieran called, bursting into his room.

"Yes?" I answered, smiling bemusedly at his at his excitement.

He let his pants fall around his ankles and asked, "Where were we?"

"Right about here," I said, pulling my dress over my head.

Kieran perused my naked body with a half-smile. "I feel guilty for asking you to marry me."

"That's because you are guilty ... of many things," I told him. "But luckily for you, I'm attracted to wicked men."

"What about reformed wicked men?" he asked, walking to the dresser to retrieve a tiny blue velvet box.

"Those, too."

Opening the box with slightly trembling hands, he asked, "Sapphire, will you consent to wear my ring?"

"With pleasure," I answered honestly, with what felt like a hundred butterflies fluttering madly in my stomach. He already had an engagement ring? Until this moment, I doubted the sincerity of Kieran's sudden proclamation of love, but now, I knew beyond the shadow of a doubt that he loved me. Like, really loved me. Forever was … well, forever.

"Pleasure?" He arched an eyebrow as he slipped a perfectly sized diamond and sapphire cluster on my finger.

"You heard me."

Lifting me bride-style into his arms, he said, "I believe the king would be proud of what's about to take place in his bed."

"What's going to happen?" I asked coyly.

Kieran growled as he covered me with his body. "What isn't going to happen?"

***

As I walked the last block to my house from Kieran's, it was hard to keep my spirits up. Yes, the proposal still had me floating on cloud nine, but it was really discouraging to see how few houses decorated for the holidays this year. Every year, it was a little less, and I feared it would be long before my little gingerbread house would be the only one decorated. Maybe I could convince Kieran to decorate the square for the holidays.

That thought kept me going until I stood in front of my house. There, the last of the smile left my face as it morphed into grim determination. I'd never been afraid of my house before, and I'd be damned if I was going to start now. I wasn't going to live in constant fear in my own town, and that shit went double now that I was scheduled to marry its creator.

Steeling myself, I carefully climbed the slippery stairs to the porch and mentally prepared myself to unlock the door. The rational part of my brain knew that it was highly doubtful that someone would be waiting inside to spring on me as soon as I entered, especially during the daytime hours, but the paranoid, delusional side was screaming, "You're an idiot! Don't go in there!"

Once unlocked, the door swung open with its familiar creak. I tiptoed inside, and the first thing I noticed upon entering was the smell of burnt couch that still lingered in the air. The second thing I noticed … the new UV windows. Somehow Kieran had made good on his promise to put in new windows while I was at his house. He never ceased to amaze me … or infuriate me. How the hell did he manage to get in here without a key? And why couldn't he be bothered to tell me that it was happening while it was actually happening?

I shook my head. If I were able to tolerate Kieran for more than ten minutes straight, I'd have to get used to the liberties he took with the lives of everyone around him. And, who knows, maybe in time … a very, very long time, I could be a good influence on him and get him to change that, but I wasn't about to hold my breath. Getting him to change his ways would take patience, and I didn't have the best track record with that where Kieran was involved. The opposite, actually.

"Might as well get used to it," I mumbled, letting it go for now and moving on to the kitchen for a glass of water.

"Get used to what?" asked a voice behind me.

Shrieking at the top of my lungs, I spun around to find the scared man that had the change of address forms for Tobias. I grabbed a cast iron frying pan off the stove with my left hand and transferred it to my right. "What are you doing in my house?"

"Whoa," he said, holding his hands up. "No one is here to hurt you."

"Speak for yourself." I gripped the pan tighter. "What are you doing in my house?"

Losing the nice guy façade, he moved his overcoat and showed me the gun at his side. "Do as I ask, Sapphire, and you won't get hurt."

I took a good look at the man as I inquired, "What are you asking me to do?" There was something so familiar about him. The shape of his eyes, the tone of his voice, it reminded me of someone … someone I knew well … someone that I was now realizing was officially out of his fucking mind.

"I want you to walk out of this house with me without making a scene or calling for help," he answered. "Then I want you to get in the black Lexus parked down the block."

"Where are we going?" I asked, knowing what he would say before he said it.

"Ronan Seward's house."

Even though I knew what his answer would be, I was still disappointed in myself. Ronan doing this shouldn't have surprised me. How many times did vampires have to prove themselves unworthy before I took my blinders off, stopped beating around the bush, and admitted that people who were megalomaniacal assholes in life are even bigger megalomaniacal assholes in death?

I put the frying pan into the dish drainer with a sigh. "What's going to happen once we get to Ronan's?"

"That depends on you," he said cryptically.

"Fine. Let's go."

***

Once I was safely ensconced in the backseat of my kidnapper's car, and he was in the driver's seat, I asked, "So, how are you related to Ronan?"

"We're from the same country, not the same family," he answered, putting the car into gear and pulling out onto the street.

"It's not the accent that tipped me off," I persisted. "It's the shape of your eyes and the tone of your voice."

He gazed at me in the rearview mirror for a few seconds before speaking. "I'm his great-great-great-great-grandson."

"And you're his evil henchman because…"

"I'm not his evil henchman," he told me in an extremely harassed voice that was identical to Ronan's. It would have been comical if he wasn't in the middle of a felony.

"Uh, like it or not, you have a gun, and you're kidnapping me in broad daylight for someone," I told him. "That, by definition, makes you an evil henchman."

Aggravated, he shot me another exasperated look. "Listen, all I know is that my gran-da is asking me to get you. If he's doing that, there's a good reason for it. Who knows? You could be a terrorist, or a spy, or a drug smuggler for all I know."

"Or I could be a postal worker who's holding on to her house because it's all she has left in this world, even if in doing that, it means I have to live in a town where everybody hates me, wants to fuck me, or wants to kidnap me for some nefarious reason that will probably prove to be as insane as the rest of this week has been."

"Or you're a vampire slaying puppy murderer, and that's not really your house," he countered. "What did you do, kill some old lady for it?"

I sat back against the seat and seethed until we pulled into Ronan's driveway. That stupid jerk! How dare he? Talk about adding insult to injury. Kidnapping me wasn't bad enough? He had to throw a little murdering my grandmother in there for good measure?

ALL I WANT FOR CHRISTMAS ARE MY TWO FRONT FANGS

The, so far, nameless Seward spawn opened the car door and grabbed my arm as I got out to make sure I wouldn't run. Little did he know, I had no intention of running. It hadn't even crossed my mind. However, kicking him in the crotch and/or face had definitely taken center stage in my thoughts on our not so pleasant thirty-second drive. That insufferable jerk had no idea how close he came to having a stiletto-related injury after that crack about my Me-maw's house.

"Come on," he said, urging me none too gently up the walk. "Ronan is waiting."

Ronan was nowhere to be found when his asshole product of procreation ushered me inside the house, but I suspected we were being watched just the same. I looked up, and my suspicions were confirmed. There were several tiny circular cameras mounted into small recessed spaces where there used to be decorative lights installed. What was with this obsession vampires have for cameras?

"I'm so glad you could make it," Ronan said from the top of the stairs.

"Why am I here?" Clearly, he was living in delusion-land if he had talked himself into believing that I'd come here willingly.

He descended the stairs and stopped in front of me. "It's time that you become one of us."

"A Democrat?" I asked.

"A vampire," he corrected, without his customary humor.

I shook my head in disbelief. "Are you on vampire crack? Because that shit is not going to happen, Ronan."

In a flash of movement, his large hand encircled my throat. I struggled to breathe, gripping his arm with both of mine in desperation until he released me, and I fell to the floor gasping for air.

"Gran-da!" Ronan's grandson shouted. He looked horrified as

he saw me crash to the tiled entrance and stormed over to help me up, but Ronan stopped him by tossing him all the way across the room with one hand.

Towering over me, Ronan growled, "Do what I ask, Sapphire. It's for your own good."

"He didn't tell me he was turning you against your will," my would-be savior told me from his prone position. "I wouldn't have helped if I would have known."

Unmoved by his grandson's speech, Ronan spoke to him without looking away from me. "Fine. You may leave."

The man glanced down to where I crouched. "I'm sorry."

I didn't dare say a word. As much as I wanted to curse him and give him a couple choice fingers for leaving me here, there was no telling what Ronan would do to me if I made him angry. The next time he choked me could be the last time.

"You're sorry?" Ronan asked his grandson. "What are you sorry for?"

Instead of answering, his grandson lunged for the doorknob to escape. Like me, he could hear the coiled up snake slithering in Ronan's voice, and understandably, didn't want to be the one within striking distance.

If Ronan's grandson would've moved a little faster, maybe he would have made it into the safety of the sunlight, or maybe if Ronan weren't a vampire that was over ten times stronger and faster than a twenty-something human, he would have survived, but I doubted it. The speed Ronan displayed as he hastened to his kin was unbelievable, as was the vehemence in his expression as he ripped the head from his descendant's shoulders.

During the seconds it took for the gore from the head to fall onto the carpet, I was silent, unmoving in my shock. I was literally frozen in place. Then, as the body fell to the floor, I started screaming. I couldn't stop, though I desperately didn't want to draw attention to myself. For the first time in my life, I was completely hysterical. The sight of someone I'd known and trusted for over two years pulling the head off of his own descendant like he was a life-size Ken doll was burned into my retinas. I wasn't sure if I'd ever stop screaming.

Amber-eyed, Ronan looked up angrily from his kill and stalked toward me. "Shut up!" he demanded.

With tears streaming down my face, I clamped my jaw shut, but couldn't manage to stop myself from whimpering. Calm would be a distant memory for a long time, even with the threat of death looming over me.

"I said, shut your mouth," he threatened angrily, trailing his sticky, bloodied fingers down the side of my face. "Don't you understand that it's better this way?"

My voice shook as I asked, "What's better this way?"

"You and me, lass. Once you're a vampire, we can start over. There will be none of my past, none of the worries to get in the way of our love. I can wipe everything clean for you. You never have to think of any of this again."

I didn't respond, just stared straight ahead at the door keeping me from sweet, sunshiny freedom and tried to stay upright as a wave of nausea swept over me.

"Why won't you say anything?" he demanded.

"I—I'm afraid," I stuttered.

Ronan's laugh was light, carefree, despite the evil that he'd done. "My love, what do you have to be afraid of?"

"You," I said, praying he wouldn't react. "You killed your grandson. You hit Alexis."

"Sapphire," he reasoned. "They didn't want us to be together."

Not looking him in the eye, I took a deep breath and braced myself before I said, "I don't want us to be together."

He shook his head and gave me a pitied look. "You don't mean that."

"Yes, I do," I told him earnestly. "Ronan, you're my friend. I love you like a brother, nothing more."

"You can't say that to me," he spat, obviously becoming agitated. "Not after what I did for you." He pointed at the corpse of his grandson. "You did this. You caused this by whoring yourself to Kieran and Tobias. If you had kept your fucking legs shut, I could have waited. Do you know how angry I am with you for what you've caused?"

I cringed away from him. "I'm sorry. I didn't mean to upset you."

With a roar of rage, he slapped me. Pain exploded out from the point of contact before the sheer force of the blow ricocheted me into the wall. Barely conscious, my only thought as darkness crept over me was that I felt a crunch of bone in my face when I was jostled to the floor. I knew that, after today, I would never look the same.

***

The room was spinning. No, scratch that. The world was spinning. Groaning, I rolled into the fetal position, willing the motion to stop.

"Good. You're awake."

The sound of Ronan's voice brought the dizzying motion in my head to a screeching halt. How long had I been asleep? And where was I? I said a quick prayer that I was at home and tried to open my eyes. I couldn't. My face was too swollen to open them both.

"There you are," Ronan said, looking remorseful as he stood over me.

"H-hi," I stammered, wincing at the intense pain radiating from the entire left side of my face.

ALL I WANT FOR CHRISTMAS ARE MY TWO FRONT FANGS

"I have to sleep," he told me without preamble. "But before I do, I want you to know that if you try to leave this bedroom while I'm sleeping, I will kill you."

The flutter of hope I'd felt in my heart when he said he would have to sleep was immediately extinguished by his threat.

He smiled at my defeated expression. "You have nothing to fear." He reached forward to touch my face and smiled again when I couldn't stop my small, involuntary flinch. "My touch, as much as it disgusts you now, will bring you endless hours of pleasure once you're turned."

Tears slipped down my cheeks as my mind whirred. I had to think of a way out of this room, out of this house, but I knew it wouldn't be easy. Like the bedroom I was in, most of the rooms in Ronan's house didn't have any windows leading outside. Alexis told me ages ago that windows made Ronan nervous.

Nervous, my ass. It was probably more like, Ronan needed a place to store the pissed off women he kidnapped.

"I've embarrassed you with my vulgarity," Ronan surmised when I didn't say anything in response to his suggestive comment.

"No, I ..." Panic started to rise in me as I realized that my best chance at escape was the door ... the door with three fucking keyed deadbolts installed in it. I needed a plan b, but there was nothing left for me to do, except try to charm him into letting me go, and honestly, if that's what my life depended on, I'd probably be dead before suppertime. "I'm not used to hearing you say things like that," I continued lamely. "I didn't know you thought of me in that way."

"I think of you all the time," he told me with a smile. "I watch you all the time, too. I'm a wee bit obsessed."

"O-oh," I stuttered, terrified by how far he'd taken his obsession, but a little more hopeful that I'd be able to talk him into letting me leave than I was before.

"I know that the way this whole thing went down is a little unorthodox, Sapphire, but I can promise that it will be worth it in the end." When I didn't respond, he added, "Have I ever let you down before?"

"No," I lied. The truth was, Ronan was letting me down now. Not to mention, he was spouting insanity. What did he mean it would be worth it? What could be worth his grandson's life?

"I can't stand to see you like this," he said.

Silent, I trembled violently as he moved closer and reached out to touch the uninjured side of my face.

"You need help, Sapphire. Let me help you."

"O-okay."

Ronan pulled his shirt over his head and casually tossed it onto the bed. "You'll have to drink my blood to heal, but don't worry, it won't taste like blood for long. I know how much you dislike it."

Was he serious? If he knew how much I disliked it, why would he make sure I'd have to drink it for eternity? "Ronan, I need to go to the hospital."

"I can't let you leave, Sapphire. You know I can't."

"Please, Ronan," I pleaded. I was in so much pain; the insistent throbbing of my heartbeat in my cheek was almost more than I could take. I was seconds from giving in to the agony and passing out.

Without a word of warning, his hand snaked out to cruelly crush my face. I screamed. I couldn't think. All I knew was pain.

"Relax," admonished Ronan. "I wouldn't have to do this if you would just do as I ask."

Through my blurred good eye, I could see Ronan bite into his palm and bring it toward my face. Struggling weakly against his strong grip, I pushed at his chest as the taste of his blood filled my mouth. It was over. He'd won. And I knew what would come next.

ALL I WANT FOR CHRISTMAS ARE MY TWO FRONT FANGS

Ronan's eyes flashed black as he smiled at the sight of me choking on the fast flow of the poison that would make me his slave. "This will be over soon, Sapphire," he promised, letting me sink down against the headboard.

Sobbing openly, I said, "Just do it. Just end this."

Slipping one hand around my jaw and one around the back of my head, he said, "As you wish."

And then there was nothing.

***

My eyes popped open a second before I sprang out of bed. Barely stopping my momentum before I banged into the wall, I leaned my head against the cool sheetrock and inhaled. I could smell everything—the soap in the adjacent bathroom, the corpse in the living room, even Ronan's cologne from across the room. I lifted my head from the damp coolness of the wall and turned to glance at my comatose sire, hissing involuntarily when the memories of his cruelty came crashing back.

With murderous rage seething from me in waves, I stalked to his side of the bed and glared down at Ronan's peaceful face before realizing that I was wasting my only chance to escape on petty revenge. I couldn't afford revenge. This was the only opportunity I would get to kill him. If I couldn't manage to get away from him while he slept, my freedom would become a distant memory. One command from Ronan and there'd be no escaping his reach—ever.

Rushing to the bathroom with speed I was unused to, I caught myself on the sink and allowed myself a second's glance at my reflection. The swollen eye, the broken cheek, they were gone. They'd been replaced by stunningly perfect skin and a hypnotic bright green gaze. A giddy laugh escaped me. How absurd this moment was. After all of the years of wanting to fit in, I was finally a vampire, but I couldn't enjoy it unless I killed my best friend's newly psychotic husband, who'd always treated me like a little sister.

Shaking off the guilt and aversion to blood, I steeled myself for what I was about to do. I could do this. I had to do this. There was no other choice. With a surge of strength, I ripped the towel rack from the wall and broke off one end, then froze until I was sure the noise didn't wake Ronan.

Less than confident about my chances of survival, I crept across the bed with stealthy movements until I was close enough to put the bar through his heart. Trembling, I gripped the bar in both hands and prayed that I wouldn't miss. I had one chance to do this right.

An achingly loud crashing noise brought my attention up to the far wall of the bedroom. Nearly crying at my lost chance to kill Ronan, I scrambled off the bed and wedged myself between the wall and the nightstand in a fruitless attempt to hide from whatever was breaking through the wall with what sounded like an ax. Terrified, I listened as the chopping noise got louder and louder and then screamed when it broke through the sheetrock. Bright beams of daylight blinded my vision, and I sank farther down into my hiding spot. I couldn't tell whether Ronan had woken or not. Surely, he couldn't have slept through the demolition of his bedroom wall.

"Where are you, Sapphire?" Korrina's worried voice yelled from outside the hole in the wall.

As much as I wanted to answer her, I couldn't, for fear of getting caught. Ronan couldn't sleep through this much longer, could he?

"Fuck it," Korrina said to herself, then she climbed into the room looking like a warrior ready for battle. When she saw Ronan sizzling in the sun, she yelled, "There you are, you piece of shit!" before her eyes landed on me "Oh my God, Saph. Shit!" Quickly, she ran to the gaping hole in the wall to try to cover as much of the sun's rays as she could. "All the way to the car," she commanded to whoever was listening. Immediately there was a loud rumble, and the house started shaking.

"What is that, Korrina?" I asked, afraid to move.

"It's just the trees. Give them just a sec, and we'll get you out of here. They're almost done." She looked back to my face, which was bloodied with grateful tears. "Fuck, Saph, Kieran is going to murder Ronan when he sees you. He's going out of his mind out in the car."

"I'm here," Kieran corrected, in a voice that clearly said we were enjoying the calm before the storm. "Sapphire, my love, come to me."

"Kieran," I breathed, rushing into his arms.

"Don't worry. I'm taking you home." He looked behind him. "Obsidian?"

"I've got Ronan," Obsidian answered. "I'm ready when you are."

"Let's go. Korrina, after you drop us off, can you meet the police when they come to claim the body in the next room?"

"Sure. No problem." She glared over at Ronan. "Actually, it would be my pleasure."

Nodding, Kieran lifted me into his arms and ducked out of the hole to carry me through the elaborate tunnel of roots, limbs, and branches that Korrina had instructed to protect us until we got into his sun resistant SUV. The second he had me inside, Korrina jumped into the driver's seat and sped toward Kieran's house. I couldn't get there fast enough. I hadn't expected Kieran to take Ronan with us, and just being around him made me want to risk sun exposure to assure that he would never have the opportunity to make me his slave.

"Relax, Sapphire," Kieran soothed, kissing my forehead.

Wide-eyed, I looked behind us to the backseat where Obsidian sat with Ronan and said, "I can't. I have to get away from him before he wakes."

"You will. It's only one o'clock. He won't wake for at least three more hours, and with him having to heal, it may take longer."

"Okay," I finally conceded, settling into his side as he wrapped a protective arm around me. I just hoped he was right.

CHAPTER TWELVE

"I am confident that you'll be safe in my bedroom," Kieran said, showing me into the house from the garage. "But just for my sanity's sake, can you turn the volume up on the TV? Ronan may realize that you're close when he wakes, and I don't want to take the chance that you'll overhear a command that has malicious intent. Now that his plan has failed, he may try to harm you. And since he has obviously figured out a way to avoid my commands, I cannot stop him from doing so."

"Trust me," I told him. "There is nothing I would like to do more right now."

"My love, I trust you implicitly, but the community won't if they find out you're Ronan's childe. There is always a ridiculously unfounded fear of the sire's insanity transferring to his children when a vampire begins to lose their faculties."

I held up a hand. "Can you seriously never call me his childe again?"

"I'm being very serious here. No one can know apart from Korrina and Obsidian."

Kieran's protectiveness was amped up to a thousand; he was taking no chances with my freedom, and I was more than thankful, but I wasn't about to exclude my best friend from one the most significant changes in my life. "Alexis has to know."

"She's a human, Sapphire."

"Alexis has to know," I repeated firmly.

He sighed. "If you're sure you can trust her."

"It's Alexis, Kieran. We can trust her."

"If you're sure."

"I am."

"Okay," he said, looking very much not okay with it as he dug through a dresser drawer and produced a bright pink and black pair of fuzzy winter ear muffs. "When I leave I want you to put these on."

I took what he offered and held them up. "Why do you have ear muffs … women's earmuffs?"

"I have a sister," he answered defensively.

"Living?"

"Undead, but yes. You met her earlier in the kitchen."

"You're kidding? That was your sister? You could have told me!"

"And ruin this moment? Never." His fleeting smile fell as he placed the muffs over my ears and remembered what he had to do. "Promise me you'll stay in this room. No matter what you hear, stay in here. Promise me."

"I promise. When it's over, you can find me in the bathroom with the shower on."

He handed me the remote to the TV. "Good girl. This should only take a few minutes."

I touched his arm to stop him as he turned to leave. "Kieran?"

"If there were any other way, I would do it, Sapphire. There is no saving him. Once a vampire goes rogue, there is nothing to be done. Ronan is a threat to the community, Alexis, and to my beloved fiancée. He must be eliminated before he has a chance to harm someone else."

"But what about Alexis?"

"She is in full agreement. I'll explain everything as soon as I return."

"Okay," I said worriedly. "You know where I'll be."

"Until then," he said, kissing me with unrestrained passion.

"Until then," I responded. Dazed, I touched my lips and stared after him in awe.

***

I sat on the edge of the bathtub, chewing my nails and tapping a worn spot into the bathmat for about a half hour before I heard the sound of Ronan's scream of rage. Thankfully, any words he might have said were incoherent with the amount of anger and denial disguising his normal tone, the TV that was loud enough to wake the permanently dead, and the crashing sound of the water rushing out of the tub's faucet, though for a few seconds, the urge to go downstairs was overwhelming.

And then, the pain came. It attacked me from all sides and within, making me scream out with every wave of agony. At first, I was sure the pain was mine. How could it be anyone else's? But then the realization that I was feeling my sire burn to ash in the sun hit me, and though Ronan had turned me into a vampire against my will and was more cruel to me than anyone had ever been, it killed me to know that he was dying. Not just for Alexis, but also for Ronan himself. He may have had an ulterior motive for making me his childe, but in his mind, he was doing it because he cared. To him, it was the only right thing to do.

When the pain finally subsided, I knew Ronan was gone. Fat bloody tears rolled down my face, and there was a strong feeling of emptiness in my heart where the pain had been the strongest. My maker and friend were gone. Even after everything he'd put us through, after all the terrible things he'd done, I knew we would still miss him—horribly. He was once our family.

Breaking the loudest silence I'd ever heard, a very welcome, accented voice asked, "Saphir?"

I jerked my head up from my hands and yanked the ear muffs off. "Tobias?"

The vampire in question slowly opened the door, with a look

of awed surprise. "Saphir, you are … beautiful as a vampire. Your eyes sparkle with an inner light. I knew you would be amazing."

"Thank you," I answered sheepishly, noticing the absence of the usual heat in my cheeks when complimented. "Is the coast clear?"

"It is, though you may want to give Kieran a few minutes to himself." He turned off the faucet, looking thoughtful. "What he had to do is the hardest thing a maker will ever go through. He'll need some time to come to terms with it."

I nodded. I couldn't imagine what it must be like to have to kill a friend, especially one he loved enough to give the gift of everlasting life. The pain of losing Ronan must be excruciating to him.

"Sapphire?" Alexis called.

"Alexis!" I yelled excitedly, practically pushing Tobias into the floor in my haste to get to my friend. "Thank God! I've been waiting for you to call since … since … what day is it?"

"It's still Wednesday. I'm really sorry. I tried to call this morning, but Ronan had already kidnapped you."

"I'm so sorry about Ronan, Alexis."

"It's done," she said resolutely. "There's no going back and no sense in dwelling in the past. I've made my peace with it."

Resting my head against her shoulder, I hugged her until she squeaked. "I'm so glad you're okay, Alexis! I don't know what I'd do without you. And I'm glad you're here, though I don't know why you'd come back here with Ronan still on the loose."

"We just got here. Kieran hired a private plane to pick us up in New Brunswick as soon as he learned of your abduction."

Surprised at Kieran's choice of hideout for Alexis, I asked, "You were with Kieran in Canada?"

"Yeah, we … uh …" she trailed off, looking lost for words.

ALL I WANT FOR CHRISTMAS ARE MY TWO FRONT FANGS

My eyes widened. "You two are together?"

Alexis grinned like a lovesick fool. "We are! You're not upset, are you?"

"Upset? I'm thrilled!" I exclaimed, hugging her again. "Congratulations!"

"Thanks," Alexis said, beaming with pride at her new vampire boyfriend. "We didn't plan it. It just happened yesterday."

"Oh, I get it. I totally get it. That's why I'm not more surprised. Even if a woman barely knew him, she would have to be blind not to see how perfect Tobias is," I admitted, then gave a little self-deprecating laugh, presumably to make the situation even more awkward between us.

Tobias smiled reassuringly at me. "If that is true, it's a trait that we all share. Both of you are exceptional women— exceptionally beautiful and exceptionally forgiving."

"Thanks," I said, and Alexis echoed me. "Wait a minute. Does that mean you're taking my best friend to Canada with you?"

He smiled down to his new love. "No, she has consented to move in with me here in Everlast."

I grinned with excitement. "That means that we're going to be neighbors, Alexis. Are you sure you're ready for that kind of commitment with me?"

"Shouldn't you be asking yourself that question?" she answered. "And besides, how long will we really be neighbors?"

Confused, I asked, "What do you mean?"

She held out her hand for mine. I reluctantly gave it to her. I knew what she'd say—the same thing I'd been saying to myself since I said I'd marry Kieran. Are you out of your freaking mind?

Looking from the billion-carat ring to my face, Alexis asked, "Is this what I think it is?"

"Yes," I said, sighing hopelessly. "I've joined the dark side."

"Honey, I could see that by the horror makeover and the fangs. This is much bigger."

"Fangs?"

She arched a well-groomed eyebrow. "Fangs."

I slapped a hand over my mouth. "I'm sorry," I mumbled. "I didn't realize. Tobias, how do I put them away?"

"You feed."

Horrified, I looked from him to my best friend in all the world and cringed. "No!"

Tobias burst into laughter. "Relax, Saphir. It's just your nature. Your fangs are only out because she's a human. Trust me, you won't bite her. You don't think of her as food. You aren't even tempted."

"How do you know?" I asked, skeptical of his blasé attitude about me potentially eating his girlfriend.

"She had to remind you that you had fangs," he said, shaking his head. "It doesn't get less interested than that."

I nodded, relieved that Alexis wasn't in any danger.

"Thanks for not wanting to make a meal of me, bestie."

"Don't mention it … ever."

"Fine, then how about this one? I am completely jealous of your complexion. Have you looked at yourself? You look amazing."

"Jealous? You? For the first time ever, I bet," I sassed. "And anyway, no matter how much I've improved, I'll never be half as beautiful as you."

"Nope, you're both perfect," Tobias interjected. "Polar opposites, but perfect. Remember, ladies?"

I rolled my eyes, which was a very peculiar feeling now that I was undead. "Speaking of perfection…"

ALL I WANT FOR CHRISTMAS ARE MY TWO FRONT FANGS

Alexis laughed and accepted the kiss Tobias bestowed upon her. "When you're right, Saph, you're right."

I smiled at the new couple's affection for each other and sighed. What a genuinely bizarre twenty-four hours this was turning out to be. I'd been engaged, was kidnapped, had my first ever bone broken, was forced to drink blood, and then I was killed. Meanwhile, Tobias and Alexis looked gorgeous together and were obviously more in love than Romeo and Juliet had ever been.

"Can I have a moment alone with Sapphire?" Kieran asked, suddenly rushing into the room.

"Of course, sire," Tobias said, ushering Alexis toward the door.

"We'll be at Tobias' house," she said, before aiming a saucy wink in my direction.

As soon as the door was closed behind Tobias and Alexis, Kieran seized my upper arms in his firm grip. "This will never happen again. I don't care what I have to do to ensure it—assign guards, get a dog, teach you taekwondo—whatever it takes to keep you safe, I'll do it. I can't lose you. I love you."

"I love you, too, Kieran, but I don't think it's possible for this particular incident to happen again."

"A chéadsearc, I thought he would wake before I was able to get to you. If Korrina hadn't been in town..." He froze for a second then cupped my face in both of his hands. "You said you loved me, didn't you?"

"I thought you missed that," I said, grinning at his reaction. The relief in his countenance was palpable.

"I've waited two long years to hear you say those words. I didn't think they would mean so much to me, but they mean everything. You are my everything, and I don't want to have to go through another night alone. Marry me tonight, Sapphire. We'll drive to Arlington after dusk. I have a friend there who will perform the ceremony."

Speechless, I gaped at him for a few seconds then asked, "Can I take a shower first?"

"Of course, you can!" Stricken, he steered me into the bathroom. "Forgive me. I am not myself today."

"After what you had to do, there's no need to apologize. It must have been horrible for you. I'm so sorry that you had to lose a childe."

"Ronan has been exhibiting signs of madness for years. I just didn't realize how close to the edge he really was. If I had known, I would have never given him the okay to marry Alexis. I certainly wouldn't have let him make plans to change her. Thank God she put it off for so long."

"It's not your fault," I said, trying to soothe him, although I knew it was an impossible task. "You didn't know."

Irritated at himself, he shook his head. "Yes, but that is exactly the point. I should have known. It's my job to control an entire region of vampires, and I couldn't keep a childe of my own from murdering my fiancée. It's appalling. It's disgraceful. Will anyone take me seriously after this?"

"Besides the six of us, are you going to tell anyone else about Ronan's death?"

"No."

"Well, then no one has to know he turned me. I'll tell everyone that you're my maker. Technically, it's true. Ronan was only a vampire because you turned him. He couldn't have made anyone without you."

Smiling, he kissed the palm of my hand. "I could have cost you your life, and I don't deserve you, but I'm going to take you up on that."

"What kind of businessman would you be if you didn't?"

The corners of his mouth perked up. "An honest one?"

"For a vampire, you're pretty honest," I said. "Don't beat yourself up too bad about it." When those words didn't seem to have an effect, I added, "I wouldn't lie for you if I didn't think you were worthy, Kieran."

"That, alone, is keeping me sane," he confided. Sighing, he said, "I've kept you from your bath for too long. I'll leave you to it."

"Come with me?" I asked. I didn't want to be alone, and if I was being truthful, I didn't want him to be alone either. He was right; he wasn't himself today. The worried furrow between his brows hadn't left his face since I first saw him at Ronan's, even though there was nothing left for him to do but mourn the loss of a friend.

"I would love to," he said apologetically. "But I have to meet with the human authorities soon. They'll want proof the vampire responsible has been punished for his misdeeds. That means collecting the ashes and pulling the security feed."

"I understand. Go do what you have to do."

He smiled down to me and gave me one last hug, holding onto me for a few seconds longer than he could have. "I love you. I'll see you soon."

I waited until he was a few steps away before I called, "Kieran?"

"Yes, a chéadsearc?"

"I'll marry you tonight … and every night for the rest of our lives if that's what you want."

"There is nothing I want more," he assured me, stepping closer. "Nothing."

I swallowed dryly, a little nervous at the sudden intensity he displayed. "Are you okay?"

"I hardly know, but I can promise you that by this time tomorrow, I will be." He bent down to claim a soft, sweet kiss from my lips. "There are t-shirts in the dresser in the closet. We'll get some of your own clothes after dark."

"Thanks for everything, Kieran."

"It's my pleasure, Sapphire. Never forget that."

***

I'd taken thousands of showers in my lifetime. They were all pretty much the same. I always started with washing my face, then my hair, and then the rest of me. But my first post-vampire shower was different. It was an entirely new experience. Because of my sensitive skin, the rivulets of water traced my body with thousands of tiny caresses. It was ecstasy, but it was almost too much to bear. I was in complete sensory overload. Quickly stoppering the tub, I turned the shower off and started running a bath. With my heightened senses, it would be a while before I adjusted to the new feel of a shower. The temperature of the water, the feel of the jets, and the sound of the droplets hitting the tiles made everything much more intense than I was used to, and it made me wonder what else I wouldn't be able to handle. I hoped to hell it wasn't sex.

Kieran returned to his bedroom a few minutes after I finished my bath. He was silent for a few moments as he took in the sight of me in his t-shirt then handed me a glass of what I hoped was really concentrated wine. I sniffed the contents. Nope, not wine.

Wrinkling my nose, I said, "Kieran, I don't think I can drink this."

His expression was distraught. "You have to. You will waste away quickly if you don't drink."

"Fine," I muttered, unhappily taking the glass. This had to be the most disgusting thing I'd ever been asked to do.

Pinching my nose, I threw back the contents and tried not to gag. It wasn't that it tasted terrible. On the contrary, it tasted delicious. But no matter what it tasted like, blood was blood and drinking it was totally revolting.

"Thank you,"' Kieran said, taking back the glass. "I'll rinse this out."

"No, thank you," I told him sitting back down on the bed. "I knew I'd have to do it. I just didn't know how hard it would be."

Kieran studied my face, took a deep breath, and crumpled in front of me. Two fat tears of blood rolled down his cheeks before he hastily wiped them away. Mortified, he whispered, "I apologize," and turned away from me.

"Kieran, are you okay?" I asked, jumping up from where I sat and speeding to him with a tissue from the bathroom.

He accepted the tissue with another deep sigh. "Forgive me. I'm wrecked. I'll be fine tonight after I rest."

With both of mine, I grabbed his hand and pulled him to the bed with me. "Sleep with me. Everything else can wait until tonight, can't it?"

Going willingly, he let me take off his suit jacket and tie, while he kicked off his shoes and loosened the cuffs of his shirt. He was exhausted. I could certainly relate. Today had felt like the longest day of my life, and it was only three in the afternoon. Climbing into bed together, we held each other close and stared at one another in silence until we both fell asleep.

***

My eyes sprang open the second the sun went down. It was like my new body had an internal clock. Instinctively, I knew that I would be safe. Doubly so, since I was still firmly held in Kieran's protective arms.

"Good evening," he said, noticing that I was awake.

"Good evening," I replied. "Did you sleep well?"

"It may have been the best sleep I've had in a hundred years."

"Hmmm … me, too. I must have gone out like a light. I don't even remember falling asleep."

A smile stretched across his face. "I watched you. You looked like an angel."

"You've been awake for one minute, and you're already complimenting me?"

He slid his hand up my arm to my tangled hair. "You will hear nothing but compliments from me for the rest of your life, a chéadsearc."

Letting my hand wander into the waist of his boxers, I replied, "I'm looking forward to it."

"It?" he asked, arching an inquisitive brow.

"It," I confirmed, letting him roll me to my back as he moved us into the missionary position.

"Sapphire, I am seven-hundred and sixty-four years old, and every time we're together, I feel like a novice. I want to please you, but I worry I don't have it in me."

"Trust me," I told him with a smile. "You know how."

Giving me a gratified smile, he said, "You flatter me. However, I meant pleasing you on a broader scale. I want to make you happy in every way."

"And you do," I promised him, slipping my hands around his shoulders and moaning in pleasure when I felt him brush against me.

Capturing the next moan with his mouth, he surged into me. I arched off the bed. Sex with Kieran had always been a life-changing experience, but this was something altogether different. This was … like breathing—necessary to live. It was everything, and it was nothing. It was the beginning of something special and the end of what we'd had before. It was our future and our past. It was a connection—a real connection, as if we were on either end of a string stretched taut between us.

Kieran stared into my eyes, transfixed. "Be my wife, Sapphire."

"Tonight," I reminded him.

Focused like I'd never seen him, he searched my face with a look of awed relief. "Sapphire, you've made me a very happy man."

"Good," I said, before crying out, the sharp tremors of pleasure edging me closer to what I'd been aching to feel since the last time he and I were together.

Kieran was quick to follow me, growling out his release with closed eyes and gritted teeth, a deep line of concentration etched into his forehead.

Without a need to catch our breath, Kieran rolled us until I straddled him and tucked my hair behind my ears. "You are so beautiful."

"And, apparently, I make you a happy man," I said, smiling at the way he was twirling a curl of my hair around his finger.

"Yes, a very happy man," he agreed."

With a ridiculously hopeful outlook on my future and a heart full of joy, I kissed my fiancée. "I'm happy, too. You're the best Christmas present I've ever gotten."

Chagrined, Kieran slapped his forehead and groaned. "It's Christmas Eve, and I haven't bought you a gift."

How adorable was this man? Not only was he smart and giving, but he also loved me—really loved me. I couldn't ask for more from a future husband and mate.

"I already have what I want," I said, and I meant it. "You're all I want for Christmas."

Threading his fingers into my hair, he gently brought my

mouth to his. "I love you, Sapphire Dragulj."

"I love you, Kieran ..." I trailed off as I heard familiar chanting start in the front yard.

What do we want?

Vampires only!

When do we want it?

Now!

Laughing as I shook my head, I asked, "You mailed the expansion notices, didn't you?"

Kieran pressed his lips together to hide his grin. "Why do you ask?"

I groaned. "Are you going to say anything to them?"

"Not tonight, a chéadsearc. Tonight, we start our forever."

THE END

Books by J.D. Nelson

Wicked Ways Series

A Night of Wickedness
All I Want For Christmas Are My Two Front Fangs: A Wicked
Ways Companion Novel
Wolves Will Be Wolves
Too Cute To Spook: A Wicked Ways Companion Novel

Night Aberrations Series

Night Aberrations
The Fire within the Night

Tales of Desire

Control

Havenwood Falls Sin & Silk Novellas

Plans Laid Bare
Soul Laid Bare

About the Author

JD Nelson is a Bestselling Author of Fantasy Romance and Adult Paranormal Romance. An avid time-waster, JD enjoys watching TV and listening to audiobooks when she really should be writing. JD loves to hear from her readers. You can contact her through her website, AuthorJDNelson.com, or on Facebook, where she spends an alarming amount of time chatting with her many Author and reader friends, much to the dismay of her continually neglected manuscripts.

JD Nelson's Facebook
www.facebook.com/NightAberrations
JD Nelson's Twitter
https://twitter.com/authorjdnelson
JD Nelson's Facebook Fan Page
www.facebook.com/JDNelsonsNightAberrations
JD Nelson's Fan Club
http://www.facebook.com/groups/269730583130725/

www.ingramcontent.com/pod-product-compliance
Lightning Source LLC
Chambersburg PA
CBHW060220180626
46813CB00007B/2904